A NOT SO WHITE CHRISTMAS

Brandon walked up the driveway of his house and saw a light on in the garage. He found his father standing with his hands on his hips, glaring down at boxes of Christmas lights.

"What's happening, Dad?"

"Oh, hi, Brandon." Mr. Walsh seemed distracted. He picked up a strand of lights and appraised it without joy.

"Lot of work putting up that stuff. Can I help?"

"It's not the work that bothers me, Brandon. It's the fact that these bulbs are all we have."

Brandon had a bad feeling about this. Dad was generally a pretty moderate, conventional kind of guy, but every so often he went crazy, like when he'd bought that electric chord organ and played popular songs of the fifties till the rest of the family couldn't stand it and they bought him a set a headphones. Or the time when Brandon's basketball record became the most important thing in his life. Only Brandon's quitting the team to get a job had made Dad normal again.

"It seemed like enough in Minneapolis," Brandon said.

"That was Minneapolis. Christmas seemed more natural. For one thing, we had snow. Here, we have to work at celebrating."

Don't miss these books in the exciting
BEVERLY HILLS, 90210 series

Beverly Hills, 90210

Beverly Hills, 90210—Exposed!

Beverly Hills, 90210—No Secrets

Beverly Hills, 90210—Which Way to the Beach?

Beverly Hills, 90210—Fantasies

And, coming soon

Beverly Hills, 90210—Two Hearts

Published by
HARPERPAPERBACKS

'TIS THE SEASON

A novelization by Mel Gilden based on an episode with teleplay
by Steve Wasserman & Jessica Klein and story by
Steve Wasserman & Jessica Klein and Michael Swerdlick, and
an episode written by Darren Star.

HarperPaperbacks
A Division of HarperCollins Publishers

HarperPaperbacks   *A Division of* HarperCollins*Publishers*
10 East 53rd Street, New York, N.Y. 10022

Copyright © 1992 by Torand, a Spelling Entertainment Company
All rights reserved. No part of this book may be used or reproduced in any manner whatsoever without written permission of the publisher, except in the case of brief quotations embodied in critical articles and reviews. For information address HarperCollins*Publishers*,
10 East 53rd Street, New York, N.Y. 10022.

Front and back cover photos by Timothy White
Insert photos by Timothy White and Andrew Semel

First printing: November 1992

Printed in the United States of America

HarperPaperbacks and colophon are trademarks of HarperCollins*Publishers*

❖ 10 9 8 7 6 5 4 3 2 1

Contents

1

It's back

IT WAS BEGINNING TO LOOK A LOT LIKE Christmas.

Brenda Walsh sighed as she walked through the crowded halls of West Beverly Hills High School with her friends Kelly Taylor and Donna Martin. "Jingle Bell Rock," broadcast from the campus radio station, gave a background rhythm to every move they made. The members of some school committee she had barely been aware of were putting up what her mother called *decking*: long garlands of red or green or silver tinsel, smiling cardboard Santas, smiling cardboard reindeer, and wreaths that looked as if they were made from real pine branches (Brenda was afraid to find out for sure); they were also putting up blue and white Hanukkah decorations: squarish tops and candelabra.

Christmas vacation was only a week away, and Brenda was glad to see the decorations were going up at last. She really liked Christmas—was kind of a Christmas junkie, in fact—but this time of year always made her a little melancholy, too.

Summer past and summer future both seemed an eternity away—school would go on forever. Dylan McKay had returned from Hawaii, where he'd evidently come to some kind of understanding with his mother; he didn't talk much about what had happened. Brenda had missed him, but with the round of parties, drama class, and hanging at the beach, she'd managed to distract herself from brooding about him too much. Next summer? Who knew?

At the moment, days were short and getting shorter, and even here in Beverly Hills the nights could be nippy, giving one plenty of time to sit before a fire and think winter-long thoughts while sipping a hot spiced apple cider.

Of course, the city of Beverly Hills began to look a lot like Christmas sometime around Labor Day. In the posh shop windows on Rodeo Drive cards appeared; they were printed with sly reminders to get one's shopping done early, and accompanied by cotton snow, a splash of scattered diamonds, a Christmas bauble, and a sprig of plastic holly. The official city decorations didn't go up till Thanksgiving or even a little later, but in the malls and in the Golden Triangle downtown, Christmas began very early indeed.

The sighting of the first Christmas display of the year was always exciting, but it made Brenda a little sad, too. Christmas was becoming so commercial. She liked to give and get presents, of course, but the message of "Peace on Earth, good will toward men," seemed sometimes to get lost in the shuffle of credit cards.

But the real problem with Christmas in Beverly Hills, as far as Brenda was concerned, was that the weather was so warm she didn't have any excuse to get out the thick winter sweaters that had been such a comfort back in Minnesota. Actually, if one were to be *completely* honest, the lack of sweaters was not the problem. The real problem was the food.

Back in Minnesota, Brenda could pig out all winter, camouflage her bloated body with bulky sweaters, and then in the spring begin her slimming. By summer, when she burst from her wool and polyester cocoon, she looked moderately terrific. But in Beverly Hills, you couldn't hide inside sweaters, so you couldn't pig out, so you had to really watch yourself with the Christmas cookies, and with the candy that seemed to appear everywhere like toadstools, and with second helpings of anything. It wasn't fair. Her brother Brandon seemed to have no trouble keeping his weight down. Of course, he never wore tights, either.

Even Kelly spoke about the problems of maintaining her figure during the Christmas season. But Donna had a metabolism like a house a-fire. She could eat any amount of anything and burn it off just walking upstairs. Brenda shook her head. "What?" she said.

"Earth to Brenda. I said I would be glad when finals are over," Kelly said.

"How do they expect us to study when we have Christmas shopping to do?" Donna asked.

Shopping, yes. So many presents, so little cash. Don't think about it. Think about getting through the semester without causing any permanent damage to your grade point average. "Two more finals tomorrow," Brenda said. "That's it for me."

"Finals are so depressing," Donna said. "Let's talk about something *really* important, like what we're going to wear to the holiday dance on Friday night."

Kelly laughed and said, "*You* can wear a big sign that says, 'I came with David Silver but we're not really a couple.'"

"That's mean," Donna said.

"But fairly humorous," Brenda said. Donna had been allowing David to hang around since one of the grunion parties the summer before, and his constant presence was getting tiresome. David wasn't a bad person, and he was actually kind of cute, but he was also very young and something of a geek. He must be thinking that it was mucho exciting to be seen with an older woman such as Donna. The humorous part was that Donna kept denying they were anything more than friends.

"I don't think it's funny at all," Donna said petulantly.

"Oo, touchy," Kelly said. "You guys must be getting serious."

"I told you, Kelly. We're just friends."

This declaration reduced Brenda and Kelly to helpless laughter.

"Jingle Bell Rock" ended and for the first time, Brenda and her friends heard the disc jockey. It was David Silver.

Over the air, David said, "I dug out this old Richie Valens song because, well, because it's a great song."

The girls waited to hear what the song might be. Donna appeared to be uncomfortable, and even Kelly was curious. To Brenda, David's voice sounded like the Voice of Doom. She imagined some movie alien with David Silver's voice saying, "People of Earth! I have chosen Donna Martin to return to Venus with me as my bride."

The song began. It was a little ditty called "Donna."

Donna Martin was horrified.

"Just friends. Right," Kelly said.

Brandon Walsh, Brenda's twin brother, sat on a cold cement step of the humanities building reading his American history book. Sometimes he thought about history, sometimes he thought about how cold the step was, and sometimes he just thought. He read his book with a certain sense of controlled hysteria: It was imperative that he review as much of this stuff as he could; his final exam would take place in less than an hour.

History, Brandon decided, was really interesting, but it was also full of bits. It was the bits—the names, the dates, the places—that were the problem. He studied regularly, and was fairly sure that he had a handle on this stuff, but he wouldn't know for sure till he saw the test questions, and then it would be too late.

All by itself, his mind leaped over the history final and into Christmas vacation. His only responsibilities would be to work at the Peach Pit and to participate in certain Walsh Christmas traditions: the buying of the tree, the wrapping of the gifts, hanging the stockings by the chimney with care. He enjoyed Christmas, and even his shifts at the Peach Pit would seem relaxing after the frantic pace of his prevacation school schedule. Regretfully, Brandon yanked his mind back to the business at hand. History. The Wright Brothers. Teapot Dome. The War To End All Wars. Yeah, right.

"Big dance Friday night, B. You going?"

Brandon looked up and saw Steve Sanders leering down at him. Steve was a tall guy with curly blond hair. He presented himself as one cool dude with a rude mood. He had a smart mouth, and he generally gave the impression that he believed rules were for other people.

Brandon was amazed that despite Steve's occasionally abrasive manner, he was one of Brandon's best friends. Steve was fun to be with, something of a wild card in Brandon's otherwise quiet, stable life. Besides, Steve's hard edge protected a mushy soft interior. He could be a sensitive guy when he allowed himself the luxury.

"Is there a dance Friday night?" Brandon asked innocently. One needed to be asleep or dead not to know about the dance. Hall posters and school memos had spoken of little else for weeks.

"Look alive, Walsh. This is the Christmas blowout!"

"I'm not going."

"Why?"

"No date." Andrea Zuckerman would probably have accepted his invitation, but Andrea was a different can of live bait altogether. He liked Andrea. He really did. But she was more of a friend than a girlfriend, and Brandon wanted to keep it that way, at least for the moment. No, inviting Andrea would be a big mistake.

"Date optional, Walsh. Minus points for a lame excuse," Steve said.

Brandon needed to get back to World War I. Talk of dances and parties made him nervous. He didn't make small talk, he didn't drink alcohol, and he didn't dance. He could meet women at school or at the Peach Pit. At parties, everybody's intentions were just a little too obvious. "I'll make this real clear for you, Steve," Brandon said, "I don't have a date *and* I don't dance. I don't waltz, rumba, foxtrot, cha cha, lambada, or boogie. I don't dance, don't ask me. I do not now, nor have I ever had Saturday night fever. I don't even like being in the same room with people who are dancing. Is that perfectly clear?"

Steve's exasperation showed in his face and in his wild arm motions. "Brandon, it's just called a dance. You don't actually have to dance. As a matter of fact, I've seen you dance, and I suggest that you stick with drinking punch and cruising."

It occurred to Brandon that something was going on here. Steve would not be so eager to find out what Brandon's intentions were unless they somehow affected Steve. With a feeling of resignation, Brandon asked Steve if he was going to the dance.

Offhandedly, as if it meant less to him than David Silver's existence, Steve said, "Yeah, well, actually, I was thinking of breaking down and asking Kelly. I think she deserves another chance."

"You're giving *her* another chance? Isn't she the one who dumped *you?*"

Steve shrugged and said, "Yeah, well, it was just a lapse in judgment. I forgive her."

As if on cue, Kelly walked by. Brandon

watched as Steve stalked her for a moment, and then put his hands over her eyes. She stopped short. "Guess who?" Steve asked.

Kelly smiled and said, "Hello, Steve."

He took his hands away and she turned to him, friendship personified. Evidently, she was in her "Steve is my friend" mode, rather than her "Steve is a vile creep" mode, or even, "Steve is my enemy" mode. Brandon could never predict which Kelly he was going to see, and he suspected that Steve never knew either.

"What gave me away? My scent? My warm and sensuous touch?" Steve asked.

"Your sweaty palms?"

"Be nice or I'll go away." He shook a playful warning finger at her.

"You're making this too easy," Kelly said and turned to leave.

Steve put a hand on her shoulder and said, "Okay. Friday night. The big dance. You and me. What do you say?"

Brandon would swear that Kelly appeared to be pleased when she said, "I'm sorry. I already have a date."

"So break it."

"I can't."

"Why not? Who are you going with?"

For the first time, Kelly seemed a little nervous, perhaps even unhappy that she was going with somebody else. "Chuck Wilson," she said.

Steve was astonished. Brandon didn't understand. As far as he knew, Chuck Wilson was just some guy around school. Brandon had never had much to do with him, and as far as he knew, neither had Steve.

Angrily, Steve said, "Nice thing to tell me just before I take my history final. You picked the one guy you knew would really get to me, didn't you?"

"What was I supposed to do? He asked me."

"Of course he did. He knew you'd tell *me*."

"You know, Steve, you're not the center of everybody's universe. What makes you think Chuck was thinking of you when he asked me to the dance?"

Brandon noticed that Kelly had slipped into "Steve is a vile creep" mode. And Steve's emotional outpouring was becoming more intense. He wasn't angry at Kelly, but he wanted to make certain she understood.

"I know he was thinking of me because I know him," Steve said. "Boy, do I know him. Believe me, he doesn't care a thing about you."

"Steve, why is it that every time a guy likes me, you try to ruin it?" Kelly wasn't understanding. She was just hurt. She'd opened up to Steve, and he'd shut her down. Brandon didn't even know why she still kept a "Steve is my friend" mode except that sometimes they did act like friends. For them, jealousy was a sometimes thing.

"To me, Chuckie Wilson isn't just any guy," Steve said.

"Well, I'm going to the dance with him whether you approve or not. At the moment, I have a final to take. Good-bye."

Kelly was not a large girl, but she managed to stomp off with the attitude of Arnold Schwarzenegger. Steve came back to Brandon's cold step and sat down next to him. He bit the tip of his thumb while he thought. Brandon wanted to ask questions, but he also wanted to give Steve some space. After all, what happened between Steve and Kelly, or between Steve and Chuck Wilson (whoever he was) was none of Brandon's business.

Suddenly, Steve cried, "Damn it! If I flunk history, you can thank Chuckie Wilson for me."

"I don't get it, Steve," Brandon said. "What is Chuck Wilson to you?"

Steve looked at Brandon with amazement and disgust. He said, "You don't watch nearly enough television. Come over to my house after school, and I'll show you."

"I'm there," Brandon said.

The history final was not as bad as Brandon imagined it would be. He was surprised how many bits he remembered. After school, he went over to Steve's house. Steve drove them in his black Corvette, silently, grimly. A few times, Brandon tried to make conversation, but Steve only replied, "You'll see. I'll show you Chuckie Wilson."

Steve lived in a big white house, about average for a Beverly Hills pile. He left his 'Vette in the driveway and took Brandon upstairs to his room. It was a nice room, neat but not fussy, with a few sports posters on the walls. Brandon got the feeling that Steve had been living in this room for a long time, since he was a little kid, maybe.

"Pull up a chair, old son, the show is about to begin." He turned on the TV, and Brandon was treated to snow and static. Steve selected a video-tape, and with an angry flourish, shoved it into the VCR. As the tape began, Steve plopped onto his bed and crossed his arms.

A moment later, to Brandon's surprise, an episode of "The Hartley House" began. He knew that Steve's mom, Mrs. Sanders, had been a TV mom in the seventies, and he'd actually seen the show a couple of times. But generally, he pre-ferred "Star Trek" reruns or sports. "The Hartley House" always seemed vapid and dumb. The relentlessly jolly theme music came up, and then the credits:

SAMANTHA SANDERS as MARY JO HARTLEY
CHARLES WILSON as CHUCKIE HARTLEY

There, behind the words, was little Chuckie bouncing on Mary Jo's knee, and both of them laughing like idiots.

"That's Chuck Wilson?" Brandon asked. "That dorky kid on your mom's TV show?"

"None other. And he's as obnoxious now as he

was then. Got himself thrown out of practically every private school in L.A."

"So now West Beverly has to deal with him."

"Right. Watch this," Steve said as he grabbed the remote and thumbed up the sound.

Grinning like a tiny demon, the five-year-old Chuckie tiptoed into the dining room, where a big colorful birthday cake stood in the center of the table. If the canned laughter was any indication, the audience was really enjoying the performance.

"Why are we watching this?" Brandon asked.

"Just watch," Steve said.

Chuckie arrived at the table and reached across the open space as if to swipe some frosting with his index finger. But there was too much table between him and the cake—he couldn't reach. With each attempt, Chuckie got a bigger laugh.

Brandon was only mildly amused. The gag was hardly in the same league as anything done by the Marx Brothers, or even by the Three Stooges. He didn't understand why Steve was bothering to show this to him.

Chuckie climbed onto a chair and reached for the cake with both hands. He pulled it toward him, lost his balance, and with a squawk, fell face first into the top of the cake. The canned audience had never seen anything so funny.

Mary Jo strode into the room and cried, "Chuckie! What are you doing?"

Chuckie lifted his frosting-covered face and

showed it to the camera. He looked like the kid in the moon. The audience went wild. "Hi, Mom," Chuckie said innocently, as if his face were not covered with evidence.

"But that cake's for your daddy's birthday!" Mary Jo said. She sounded more surprised than upset, as if she'd never dreamed Chuckie could be so clever.

"I was just testing it. To make sure it was good enough for Daddy."

The audience loved that as much as Mary Jo, and they applauded when she hugged him.

"I think I'm going to puke," Steve said. He fired the remote at the TV, and the screen went black.

"I don't get it, Steve. He was just some stupid kid. What does this have to do with you and Kelly and the dance?"

"Listen, Brandon: When I was little, I used to go to the studio to see my mom. And they'd stick me and Chuckie together, you know, because we were the same age. He'd hit me, pull my hair, bite me, break my toys, and every time, I'd be the one who got blamed."

"Why?" He could see that Steve was building to something here, but Brandon didn't know what.

"He was a star, Brandon. A five-year-old kid with an attitude. And if he didn't get his way, he wouldn't go on. And if he didn't go on, big big money was up in smoke. That cute little smile of his was an important commodity. Nobody much cared if little Stevie was unhappy."

"What about your mom?"

Steve shrugged. "She played along. It was all part of the job. Learn your lines, hit your marks, and be nice to Chuckie."

"But that's all ancient history. You've changed. He's probably changed, too."

"Some things never change," Steve said ruefully. "When I first saw him at West Beverly, he said, 'Watch out, Steve-o. Chuckie's back.' You know, like the ads for that horror movie?"

Steve's problem seemed like a bad movie of the week: rotten kid grows up and returns to give trouble to his old victim. Brandon chuckled and said, "'The Phantom of West Beverly High.'"

Steve went on as if he hadn't heard Brandon. In a daze, he said, "I thought he was out of my life. First, he shows up at school. Then—you'll never believe this." Steve shook his head.

"What?"

"They're talking about doing a big 'Hartley House' reunion show." He waited for Brandon to react to this bomb.

All these parts obviously fit together for Steve, but Brandon was still bewildered. "After all these years? Why?"

"Because of the Big Two factors in corporate creativity: ratings and money. Hell, Brandon, more people watched Andy Griffith go back to Mayberry than walk upright."

He saw that Steve was upset, but Brandon could not take this seriously. Trying hard not to smile, Brandon said, "Yeah, but Andy had Barney, Gomer, and Goober. Not to mention Opie, who is now a big-time director."

"Yeah," Steve said sarcastically. "And we have little Chuckie."

"I still don't—"

"He's the big holdout, Brandon. Mom and I are going to have dinner with him tonight. You know, help my mother entertain him so he'll be a good boy and sign his deal?"

A face looked in around the edge of the partly open door. It was a friendly American face framed in blond hair, and it belonged to Steve's mom, the famous and beloved Samantha Sanders. She was a little older than Brandon's mom, but well preserved and still pretty.

The smile she used on them gave off megawatts of power. "Brandon, darling, how are you? Steve, you didn't tell me we had company." Brandon didn't even flinch when Mrs. Sanders said 'darling.' It didn't sound fake and forced, but like a word a mom would use when addressing somebody she genuinely liked.

"Brandon's not company, Mom," Steve said sourly.

"Steve says there's going to be a 'Hartley House' reunion, Mrs. Sanders. Congratulations."

As far as Brandon was concerned, it was just a polite thing to say, but the words upset Mrs.

Sanders. She said, "Don't jinx it. We haven't signed the deal yet." She began to muse, to spin out her own private fantasy. "But Norman says it looks good. We may even get a TV movie." Back on Earth, Mrs. Sanders finished, "If Charles agrees to do it."

"Charles?" Brandon asked.

"Little Chuckie," Steve said with venom.

"Whatever you do, Gorgeous, do not call him that at dinner."

"Gorgeous?" Brandon asked, incredulous. Amazing, the stuff you learned hanging around other people's bedrooms.

"On second thought," Steve said, "I'm eating at Brandon's."

Brandon knew that Steve was serious, but Mrs. Sanders preferred to treat Steve's last remark as a joke. She shot Steve a worried smile and said, "I know you two have had your differences, Gorgeous, but this means a lot to me."

Steve thought that over and nodded. He wasn't happy, but Brandon suspected he would cooperate for his mom's sake. Unless Steve forgot himself and exploded. In which case, dinner that night at the Sanders home was sure to be like a head-on collision—spectacular but deadly, and not very pleasant for those most directly involved.

2

My dinner with Chuckie

BRANDON WALKED HOME FROM STEVE'S house through the fragrant streets. Funny how in Beverly Hills some flower was always blooming, no matter what time of year, no matter what time of day. The air was turning cold, and Brandon was glad to have his jacket. In Minnesota, it was his autumn jacket. Here in California, their Midwest winter stuff was put behind them, like the Midwest winter itself.

Though it was not yet six o'clock, the city was already dark and the streetlights had come on. The big white houses looked forbidding except where the occasional square of friendly yellow light hung like a picture on the wall. But this time

of year, the streetlights could not compete with
the decorations some people had already erected
on their front lawns.

In Beverly Hills, decorating did not stop with
outlining the house in colored lights. He saw
conga-lines of snowmen dancing around an old-
fashioned lamppost. One Nativity scene featured a
real donkey and a couple of real sheep. As far as
Brandon could tell, the Wise Men were plaster.
He liked Christmas, and decorating the house
was definitely part of the season, but he felt
uneasy about competitive decorating. It somehow
just missed being in the spirit.

In front of one house, a large man was setting
up a fence of big glittery snowflakes, each a foot
across.

"Merry Christmas," Brandon said as he passed.

"What? Oh, yeah. Sure. Merry Christmas to
you, too, young man." The man grunted and, as if
he were sending a vampire to final rest, he shoved
a spike with a snowflake atop it into the ground.

The snowflakes led Brandon to contemplate
what a pleasure it was not to have to shovel snow;
but without snow Christmas seemed diluted,
somehow lacking an important ingredient. He
had visions of the rich people who lived in the
hills above the flatlands of Beverly Hills bringing
in snow in big refrigerated trucks.

Across the street from the Walsh home, in addi-
tion to the old-fashioned lampposts that shed a
watery light onto the path to the front door, and the

usual outline of colored lights, a searchlight pointing at the roof picked out a sleigh with Santa in it. Santa was either waving or weaving in the light wind.

Brandon walked up the driveway of his house and saw a light on in the garage. He found his father standing with his hands on his hips, glaring down at boxes of Christmas lights.

"What's happening, Dad?"

"Oh, hi, Brandon." Mr. Walsh seemed distracted. He picked up a strand of lights and appraised it without joy.

"Lot of work putting up that stuff. Can I help?"

"It's not the work that bothers me, Brandon. It's the fact that these bulbs are all we have."

Brandon had a bad feeling about this. Dad was generally a pretty moderate, conventional kind of guy, but every so often he went crazy, like when he'd bought that electric chord organ and played popular songs of the fifties till the rest of the family couldn't stand it and they bought him a set of headphones. Or the time when Brandon's basketball record became the most important thing in his life. Only Brandon's quitting the team to get a job had made Dad normal again.

"It seemed like enough in Minneapolis," Brandon said.

"That was Minneapolis. Christmas seemed more natural. For one thing, we had snow. Here, we have to work at celebrating. Besides, I want the house to look nice for your mother. You know how she gets into Christmas."

Cautiously, Brandon asked, "What do you have in mind?"

"I don't know," Mr. Walsh said. He dropped the lights back into the box. "Just something to think about. We'll hang these over the weekend." He reached up and pulled the chain that shut off the single electric bulb.

Brandon was relieved. He'd been afraid his dad would want those lights to go up that night.

The house seemed warm and friendly after the cold of the garage. The odor of broiling steak was heady. Kelly and Brenda were setting the table while Mrs. Walsh tossed salad.

"Hi, guys. Sorry I'm late, Mom."

"Brandon! Where have you been?"

"I was over at Steve's house," Brandon said. He knew this would get a rise out of somebody.

Kelly frowned, but Brenda said, "What's happening over there?"

"Steve tells me his mom might be in a 'Hartley House' reunion show on TV."

Mr. Walsh was rinsing his hands at the sink. He said, "Oh yeah. I remember 'The Hartley House.'" He turned off the water, and as he wiped his hands, he sang, "'. . . All of them had hair of gold, like their mother . . .'"

"No, Dad," said Brenda. "That was 'The Brady Bunch.'"

Mrs. Walsh rested her salad forks, and looked off into a corner, as if a TV were there. She said, "'The Hartley House' was the one where they had two teenagers, and then one year they had a baby—"

Kelly took up the tale. "And the next season, he was suddenly three years old."

Brenda stole a lettuce leaf from the salad bowl and nibbled the edges as she said, "Today, that little boy is Chuck Wilson, student at West Beverly High. Kelly's going out with him."

Mr. Walsh grunted. He seemed to have lost all interest in the subject. He was searching for something in the refrigerator, probably for a bottle of catsup.

Brenda smiled wanly and said, "He's adorable."

"I'm sure," Mr. Walsh said as he closed the refrigerator and pawed through a cabinet.

"Don't you remember, Jim?" Mrs. Walsh asked. "When the kids were little, I used to say that Brandon looked just like little Chuckie." She opened a different cabinet and pulled out a bottle of steak sauce, which she handed to Mr. Walsh.

"Thank you, dear," he said.

"I did not look like him," Brandon cried. Where did parents get these ideas?

"Yes you did," Brenda said with delight. "You had that cute little cowlick."

"Can it, Brenda."

Brenda ignored Brandon and asked Kelly, "Is this guy really as bad as Steve says he is?"

"Look: I've known Steve and Chuck since elementary school. Just because they always wanted to kill each other doesn't mean I have to take sides. Does it?" Kelly was trying to be reasonable, but Brandon knew that by going to the dance with Chuck, Kelly had already taken sides. And if any of what Steve had told Brandon had been the truth, it was the wrong side.

Steve's stomach felt as if a nest of snakes were living inside. While he put on a clean shirt, he thought about how much he hated Chuckie. The guy was a first-rate creep—no, make that a second-rate creep. He wasn't good enough to be a first-rate anything. If it hadn't been for Mom, Steve would have had nothing to do with him, or pounded him into the ground, whichever seemed best at the time.

He shook his head. Kelly was making a big mistake going out with this dork. But she wouldn't listen to him. Oh no. She thought Steve was just trying to ruin her life. Was ever a man so misunderstood? Maybe the best thing he could do was stand back and allow Chuckie to do his dirty work. Then he could ride in like a white knight and save her.

Yeah. Steve liked that, and he embroidered on it in his mind. He began to hum the James Bond theme under his breath. The white knight angle was very appealing.

Of course, there was still the evening to get through. Brandon was right. Chuckie was just some kid, a high school kid now, but that's all he was. Chuckie was just trying to psych him out with all that "Chuckie's back" stuff. Steve refused to be a victim. He wouldn't allow the guy to crawl onto his back. Steve would be charming. Mom would do the show. And *then* he'd punch out Chuckie's lights. It would be kind of like a reward for being so good.

The front doorbell rang, and Steve was confident enough in his plan that he hollered, "I'll get it," and trotted down the stairs. He opened the door, and there stood Chuckie Wilson with a dozen roses wrapped in green cellophane. Chuckie said, "Steve, my man! How are you doing?" He smirked. That's what the cute smile had become—a smirk.

Steve was still confident, but he decided that a little needling couldn't hurt. Let off a little tension. Steve said, "Doing fine. Chuckie." Steve knew he hated it when anyone called him Chuckie instead of Chuck.

"Can I come in, or are we going to eat out here on the steps?"

Steve backed away from the door and graciously allowed Chuckie to enter. Chuckie looked the place over as if he'd just bought it and was thinking of turning it into a parking lot. "So, Steve-o, coming to the big dance on Friday?"

There he goes, Steve thought. It was none of the guy's business. Maybe Steve was taking Kim Bassinger. Or Michelle Pfeiffer. He hadn't made up his mind yet. Let Chuckie guess. "Maybe," Steve said.

"Don't be bogus, man. You have to come,"

Chuckie said too broadly. "Kelly and I will be really hurt if you don't show."

Kelly and who, mulch face? Did Kelly know Chuckie was talking about them as if they were a couple? Maybe he and Chuckie had time for a man-to-man discussion before Mom came downstairs. Steve said, "What's your problem, Chuck?" There. He'd called him Chuck instead of Chuckie. Steve felt he'd met the guy halfway.

"No problem," Chuckie said, and shrugged. He leaned into Steve and asked quietly, "So. Is it true?" His eyebrows rose and fell. And there was that smirk again.

"Is what true?"

"Is it true that Kelly Taylor is a really *awesome* first date?"

"That's it," Steve cried. "Get out!" He pointed at the front door. Imagining Chuckie dancing with Kelly was bad enough, but imagining them getting, well, intimate, was too much. The guy didn't even like her. He wanted only one thing. Well, two things, neither of them honorable. One of them was Kelly's fair white bod. The other was to torture Steve.

Chuck laughed, which only made Steve angrier. "Hey, man," Chuck said. "Chill out!"

Steve took a deep breath and attempted to be reasonable. "Look," he said, "we're not at the studio. Nobody's forcing me to entertain you anymore." Not much. Nobody except his mom and all the other people who had a stake in a "Hartley House" reunion show.

"Get real, Steve. Why do you think I'm here?"

To force Steve to entertain him? It couldn't be just a social occasion. His mom and Chuckie hadn't done a "Hartley House" for almost fifteen years, and Chuckie had never once come to visit or even called. Steve didn't know whether Chuckie wanted to do the reunion or not, but he was certain that Chuckie couldn't resist a chance to give him the treatment.

They stood there, Chuckie relaxed and smirking, Steve tense and angry. Steve could hear his heart pounding. And the stomach snakes were acting up again. He frantically tried to think of a way to get command of this situation, but nothing came. As long as his mom wanted to do the show, and they needed Chuckie to make it a success, Steve felt as helpless as he had back in the old days.

Steve heard a rustle of silk, and turned his head to see his mom making her entrance down the stairs like a queen. She looked terrific in a lime-green hostess gown that swept behind her. "Charles, darling," she cried happily. Then she saw Steve and Chuckie, and the smile on her face froze. The smile did not look real, not even as real as her TV smile. She said, "Steve: what's wrong?"

To Steve's chagrin, Chuckie spoke first. "Nothing's wrong."

"Steve?" Mrs. Sanders said.

"Everything's fine," Steve said tightly. Worry crossed Mrs. Sanders's face like the shadow of a cloud. While Steve tried to decide how much truth he could get away with, Chuckie sailed across the foyer to Mrs. Sanders and presented her with the roses. As she and Chuckie hugged, Mrs. Sanders queried Steve with her raised eyebrows. Steve, hating himself, just shrugged. He did it for his mom.

"You look fabulous, *Mom*," Chuckie said.

Cute, Steve thought. Real cute.

Mrs. Sanders seemed to like it when Chuckie called her Mom. She laughed and kissed Chuckie on both cheeks. "I'm so delighted to see you. It's just like the old days." She turned to Steve and asked hopefully, "Isn't it?"

"Yes. Just like the old days." That much was true, anyway.

Chuckie took Mrs. Sanders' arm and escorted her into the dining room. Steve trailed them, feeling like an outcast.

Dinner was the ordeal that Steve had visualized. Not only did he splash water when he tried to pour some for his mom, but he dripped gravy onto his best gray pants. Chuckie was constantly charming and witty, which enraged Steve. When someone spoke to him, Steve only grunted, afraid to say more. But when Chuckie started talking about how hard he was working in school, Steve blurted, "I guess if you don't do well, you can always climb into the teacher's lap and tell her how much you've always loved her."

Chuckie seemed surprised at this, but Mrs. Sanders was positively baffled.

Digging himself a little deeper, Steve explained, "Well, it always worked on the show."

Mrs. Sanders chuckled uneasily and said, "It's that cute smile of yours, Charles. You still have it."

"Sure," said Steve. "It's easy to have a cute smile when you still have all your teeth."

Chuckie laughed as if Steve had just said the funniest thing imaginable. Mrs. Sanders, looking a little ill, followed along.

The situation got even worse when Mrs. Sanders innocently asked Chuckie about his social life. Chuckie started a rhapsody about Kelly Taylor: about how lovely she was, how well they got along, how they had the same interests. "Steve used to date her, I believe," Chuckie said.

"Yeah," said Steve. "Before she lost her mind."

"She seems okay to me," Chuckie said, and winked broadly.

Mrs. Sanders dredged up a laugh, then shot Steve a brief but murderous stare.

The three of them sat over dessert for a while, but only Mrs. Sanders and Chuckie conversed. Steve glumly stirred his rapidly melting ice cream. Later, Mrs. Sanders walked Chuckie back to the front door. Steve stood in the dining room doorway with his arms crossed. He'd eat with the guy, but he refused to wish Chuckie a safe drive home.

"Thanks, *Mom*," Chuckie said. "Great dinner."

"Thank you for coming. Call me first thing in the morning. We still have lots to talk about."

"Definitely." He called to Steve, "I'll give Kelly your regards, bro."

Steve was too angry to say anything.

Evidently, Chuckie had not expected an answer, because he kissed Mrs. Sanders on the cheek, said, "Good night, *Mom*," and was gone in an instant.

As soon as the door was closed, Mrs. Sanders turned on Steve and said in a quiet but menacing voice, "I want an apology and an explanation for your behavior this evening. You were incredibly rude."

3

Dishing the dirt

NOBODY IN THE FOYER MOVED. MRS. Sanders was waiting for Steve to give her an answer, and Steve was attempting to gather his thoughts so he could force them out through his anger in coherent sentences.

Steve shook his head. "I can't believe this. Nothing changes. This is how it's always been—you're siding with Chuckie."

"This is business, Steven. This entire reunion show depends on Charles agreeing to do it."

"I guess that's more important than my entire life."

Mrs. Sanders studied Steve for a moment, and then smiled. It was a real smile, much nicer than the other kind. Steve was pleased to see that he'd made a dent in his mom's determination to protect Chuckie, but he refused to lighten up. He was still angry, and he had a right to be.

Mrs. Sanders said, "Steve. Gorgeous. Your life is always important to me. You know that. Why do you think I worked so much when you were a little boy? I was a single mother. I needed to take care of this family."

How bogus. "Save me the sob story, Mom. You were the star of 'The Hartley House,' and you loved every minute of it."

Mrs. Sanders smiled again. It was a quirky smile, part of the package that made her charming. Steve was in no mood to appreciate it. Mrs. Sanders said, "Well, if it's a crime to love your work . . ." She held out her wrists. "Arrest me."

"Bring it down, Mom. You're not running lines. This is real."

The charm evaporated from Mrs. Sanders's manner, and suddenly she was taking the hard line, explaining the realities of life. "Okay, fine. But do you know what this reunion show means to us? Syndication. Foreign rights. We're talking a lot of money here. Enough to pay tuition at any college that'll take you."

"Dad's got that covered."

"Oh, please," Mrs. Sanders said with disgust. "Don't start depending on *him*. You're my son, and I'm the one who's going to look out for you. That's all there is to it."

Maybe Mom was right. This was strictly business. He lived in a much larger universe than he had when he and Chuckie were five. He wouldn't be locked inside a studio all day with the guy. He didn't have to have anything to do with Chuckie. And if they met by accident in the hallway at school, Steve could be civil. He'd laugh if Chuckie talked about Kelly. He didn't owe his mom an apology, but maybe he did owe her an explanation. Steve said, "I'm sorry. Chuckie just goes out of his way to push my buttons."

"So don't let him," Mrs. Sanders said as if Steve were just being obstinate. "I know he can be difficult," she said sympathetically. "But you're the one who's always been more mature."

Yeah, right. The adults always demanded the oldest kid act like an adult. Meanwhile, the adults acted like kids.

"You've got to help me on this, Gorgeous. Please. Say you're sorry. Be nice to him. For both of us." She kissed his cheek.

Steve would rather have been nice to bathroom mold, but he allowed himself to be persuaded, at least for the moment. He nodded.

Andrea Zuckerman and Brandon were discussing a photo layout of the previous week's swim meet when John Griffin blew into the West Beverly *Blaze* office. He was a tall, thin guy who generally wore a tie to school. Brandon had the impression that John was a little on the slimy side and that he spent too much money on haircuts. When he thought about John at all, Brandon predicted the guy would grow up to be the host of one of those tabloid TV shows that covered Elvis sightings and the births of three-headed babies.

When John could not immediately get Andrea's attention, he said excitedly, "Have I got a story for you! 'Entertainment Tonight' says that there may be a 'Hartley House' reunion show, and with Chuck Wilson going to school here, I think it's worth an interview." He looked eagerly from Andrea to Brandon.

Slimy, Brandon thought. Between his feelings about John, and the stories Steve had told him about Chuckie, Brandon was not inclined to be sympathetic to John's proposal. He said, "John, you know the *Blaze* doesn't run celebrity puff pieces."

"Hello, Brandon," John said as he knocked on the air between them as if it were a wall. "You're not paying attention. This isn't a puff piece. Child stars are a weird breed. They're all either getting arrested or killing themselves or taking drugs. Sometimes all three at once. Don't you want to know why?"

"Not a burning issue in my book, John. Sorry."

"Besides," Andrea said, "Chuck Wilson doesn't seem particularly screwed up."

John chuckled at Andrea's innocence and said, "Oh no? For one thing, he was thrown out of his last three schools." He held his smile, waiting for a big response.

Brandon said, "What do you want to do, John? Turn the *Blaze* into a supermarket tabloid?"

John put his hand on Brandon's shoulder and said, "Lighten up, bro. This is a great story and you know it." He looked at Andrea and said, "I know what you're thinking. A story like this will be a lot of work for somebody. But I'm willing. I'll pull the clips, interview Chuck, interview Steve Sanders—"

"Why Steve?" Brandon asked. The very thought chilled him.

While John blocked out the headline in the air with his hands, he said, "I want to call the piece 'The Two Sons of Samantha Sanders.' You know, compare the real family with the TV family? Like it? How can you not like it?"

To Brandon's horror and stupefaction, Andrea was now nodding, seriously considering John's inflammatory idea.

"Come on, Andrea," Brandon said. "Steve's our friend. Do we really want some Geraldo wannabe dishing dirt on him?"

John smiled and asked, "What? Me dish?" and Brandon could not help thinking of Mad magazine's Alfred E. Newman.

Uncomfortably, Andrea said, "You know, John, a story like this takes a delicate touch, sensitivity, a feeling for the subject."

"I'm sensitive," John declared.

Brandon and Andrea stared at John with bored disbelief.

Brandon turned to Andrea and said, "Look,

Andrea. If you really want the *Blaze* to print this story, let me write it."

"I'm sensitive," John said again.

Andrea ignored him. She said, "Okay, Brandon. But remember: Be objective."

"No problem," Brandon said, though he knew the problem was humongous.

He picked up a reporter's notebook and a minitape recorder, and went in search of Chuckie. He knew where Chuckie's locker was, and the period was almost over. Finding him would not be a problem.

The problem was that Brandon didn't know if he had the delicacy to write this article either. He hadn't had much to do with Chuck Wilson, but he knew Chuck really had been thrown out of three schools and that he was taking Kelly to the winter dance. Did these facts prove that Steve was right about Chuckie being a creep? Or was the evidence circumstantial?

Brandon had been misled by circumstantial evidence before, and he did not enjoy the feeling. For his own sake as well as for Chuckie's, he would give fairness his best shot, trust Chuckie till trust no longer seemed appropriate. After that, the article would have to take care of itself. And Andrea would edit it anyway. Brandon felt that at least *he* would give Andrea something to work with.

Brandon thought these things as he walked down the hall. His train of thought was broken by the ringing of the passing bell. Kids poured out of classrooms. By the time Brandon got to the locker, Chuckie was already there, lobbing books into it with great bangs. Brandon took a deep breath and walked over to him.

"Chuck?" Brandon asked.

Chuck turned to Brandon. He looked pleasant enough. Brandon found himself wondering how good an actor Chuck Wilson really was.

"Yes?"

"I'm Brandon Walsh."

Chuck smiled in what seemed to be a sincere way. "Right. Your sister's a friend of Kelly's, right?"

"Right. Listen: I was wondering if I could do a profile on you for the *Blaze*."

"Me?" Chuck asked with astonishment.

"Sure. You're a celebrity."

Chuck held up both hands and said, "Please. That was a long time ago."

Chuck was not making this easy for Brandon, whose inclination was to say, "Yeah. You're right. Sorry to bother you," and walk away. But he'd volunteered to do this story, and he felt obligated to continue trying. What he actually said was, "Yeah, well, I hear there's talk of a 'Hartley House' reunion."

Chuck shrugged and said, "There's always talk. Sometimes I think Hollywood is nothing but talk."

"Still, I'm interested in what it's like to be a child star."

Chuck smiled. "You mean you want to hear

my theories about why so many of us wind up in the slammer or in rubber rooms?"

The more Chuck spoke, the more trouble Brandon had remembering what a creep he was supposed to be. For all of Steve's warnings, Brandon could not help liking the guy. "It can't be an easy life," Brandon said.

"Actually it can. I mean, I have a lot to be thankful for. I mean, I was given the kind of opportunities very few kids get."

"Good attitude," Brandon said.

"Think positive. That's what I always say." Chuck walked away—not quickly, but with a certain definiteness. Brandon walked with him and Chuck didn't seem to mind. Chuck said, "So listen: I'll have my publicist send you a bio and my press pack, and then we can talk."

This was more like what Brandon had expected. He said, "Your girl will call my girl?"

Chuck stopped and laughed while he shook his head. He said, "Sorry. I didn't mean to go all show biz on you. You free now? I don't have a class till two."

"I'll have to check my date book, but I think I can squeeze you in." When Chuck looked at him blankly, Brandon laughed. A moment later, Chuck laughed with him.

Still smiling, they walked outside looking for a semiprivate place to hold the interview. After actually talking with Chuck for a while, Brandon felt more capable of writing a balanced interview. It might even turn out to make Chuck look pretty good. Steve would be steamed, of course, but that couldn't be helped. Steve was his friend, but Brandon had to *get the story*, and write it as he saw it.

The sky was overcast with feathery gray, making the season seem more like winter, if not exactly like Christmas. Still, the air was unaccountably warm— not as warm as during summer, but warm enough to demand only a light jacket. Kids strolled across the quad, a few already holding apples in their mouths while they pawed through brown bags.

Brandon and Chuck found a stone bench under a big pepper tree, and Brandon pulled out his notebook and his tape recorder. Chuck glanced warily at the tape recorder, and Brandon asked, "Tape okay?"

Chuck thought that over, and at last said that it was.

Brandon switched on the recorder, uncapped his pen, and asked, "So, what was it like working with Samantha Sanders?"

"She was almost like a real mom to me. I mean, she kept me in line, she taught me about acting. She and Steve were like family."

Brandon had to admit that Chuck was charming, but he was laying on his rose-colored vision a little thick for Brandon's taste. Life was never that perfect. Besides, Brandon thought it unlikely that Steve was entirely inventing his problems with Chuck, or that he'd hallucinated them. There had to be *some* friction. Brandon said, "So, you and Steve got along?"

"We were like this." Chuck crossed his fingers and held them up for Brandon to see. "I loved him like a brother."

"A brother," Brandon repeated and wrote down the word brother followed by a big question mark.

Steve looked for Chuckie, and from the end of the hall, saw him at his locker talking to Brandon. They seemed to be getting along pretty well. So what? As far as Steve was concerned, Brandon could talk to anybody he wanted to. It was true that after all that Steve had told him, Brandon's behavior seemed a little odd, but Brandon probably had his reasons. If he didn't, he'd break Brandon's face.

However, at the moment, Brandon was not Steve's biggest problem. He'd promised his mom that he'd apologize to Chuckie, a feat he put up there with inventing the airplane and splitting the atom. It was difficult to do, but if he approached it properly, he might emerge with his skin intact.

Personally, Steve was disgusted with the whole deal: with Chuckie, with "The Hartley House," and even with his mom. He loved his mom, of course, but sometimes he wished she was not so preoccupied with show business. All the time he'd been growing up, even during the years she hadn't worked, she read the trades, the daily papers that reported show business news. That hadn't seemed so bad at the time, but Steve now found it easy to hate and despise anything that led him back to Chuckie, back to this time and place, back to this apology. Nobody should have to apologize for having human feelings. Sheesh.

He followed Brandon and Chuckie through the halls and outside to where they settled on a bench under a pepper tree. Now Steve saw what was going on. With notebook and tape recorder in hand, Brandon was obviously interviewing Chuckie. Steve didn't know why and he tried not to care. Probably something to do with "The Hartley House." He took a deep breath and walked over to them. Trying his best to be pleasant, he said, "Hi. Am I interrupting?" I hope.

They looked up at him, smiling. Brandon said, "No, we're just about done here."

Chuckie said, "I just told Brandon the story of my life. You were part of it."

"Unfortunately," Steve said. He didn't know how Chuckie did it, but he had an unerring sense of what would make Steve angry.

Chuckie chuckled warmly and leaned toward Brandon. Loud enough for Steve to hear, Chuckie said, "Sibling rivalry. It crops up in even the best of families."

This was so bogus. But it had to be done. Steve mentally girded himself and said, "Yeah, well. I just came over to apologize."

"For what?" Chuckie asked. Then he brightened and he grinned. "Oh yeah. It must be for acting like such a jerk last night."

Discipline, Steve advised himself. Discipline. He said, "Yeah, well. I'm sorry."

"Don't worry," Chuckie said offhandedly. "You couldn't help yourself."

Steve felt himself coming to a boil. He had to pull out now or there would be trouble. He said, "Listen: I told my mother I'd apologize. I apologized. Let's leave it at that, okay?"

For a moment, Chuckie contemplated the ground between his feet. He looked up at Steve and said, "You know, Steve-o, I was thinking, and I think I figured out what your problem is."

Terrific, Steve thought. "*You're* my problem, Chuckie." He really hated it when Steve called him Chuckie.

Chuckie turned to Brandon, and ignoring Steve entirely, explained, "Insecurity. That's his problem. He's just one big open wound."

Steve felt himself slipping. He couldn't help himself. He folded his arms and said, "Oh really? And what exactly do *I*, of all people, have to be insecure about?"

Chuckie shrugged. "It's a known fact that adopted kids are insecure."

Steve balled his hands into fists. He was so angry he could barely think straight enough to make sentences. But he managed to blurt out, "How the hell do you know that?"

"Steve—" Brandon said. Steve knew Brandon was trying to calm him, but it was too late for that. He didn't even want to be calmed.

"I've known since we were seven," Chuckie said. "Hey, everyone knew. We were all supposed to keep it quiet till *Mom* told you. I guess she finally broke the news, huh? Wonder what took her so long. You know—"

Steve was beyond caring about Chuckie's theories. Swinging both arms, he leaped at Chuckie and knocked him off the bench. He was aware that Brandon was trying to pull them apart, but he kept pounding at Chuckie, and pounding and pounding.

After what seemed like seconds, two P.E. teachers grabbed Steve and dragged him away from Chuckie. Steve was breathing hard, and he felt a little weak—he knew the show was over. But he had the satisfaction of seeing the skin around Chuckie's right eye darken. It would be quite a shiner.

The P.E. teachers marched Chuckie and Steve to the office of Mr. Chapman, the boys' vice principal. While they waited for Mr. Chapman to come out of his office and get them, Chuckie delicately probed his eye and said, "Thanks a lot, Sanders. If I wind up with a shiner, it'll look great on camera."

Steve grunted.

"Actually," Chuckie said, "if I get busted, there won't be any cameras."

"Too bad," Steve said sarcastically.

"I've been thrown out of too many high schools, Steve. My parents say that unless I keep my nose clean, no more work."

The guy really sounded bummed, but Steve was in no mood to be sympathetic.

"No big deal, right, Steve-o? Maybe not, but the pain in my eye has been causing me to consider my position here."

"Yeah?"

"Yeah. I've been thinking that it's really a waste for both of us to do time."

"Yeah?"

"Yeah. I've been thinking that you should take the rap for both of us."

"Eat it, bonzo."

"I *could* eat it, of course, but that wouldn't make Samantha very happy."

Steve couldn't help himself. He had to ask, "What has my mother got to do with this?"

"If you don't take the rap, I won't do Samantha's little reunion show. And frankly, given the way her career's going, she needs it a hell of a lot more than I do."

Despite Steve's low estimation of Chuckie, he was surprised. He said, "Isn't blackmail a little low even for you?"

Chuckie smiled sweetly and said, "Don't think of it as blackmail, Steve-o. Think of it as our little secret."

Steve felt frustrated and angry and betrayed. His mother had put him into this position, a position where he could do nothing but take it. He could not speak. He could only glower at Chuckie and hurt inside. The writhing of the snakes was terrible.

4

Ugly twists

BETWEEN CLASSES, BRENDA WAS WALKING through the hall with Kelly and Donna. The hot topic around school was the fact that Steve Sanders had clobbered local celebrity Chuck Wilson. Brenda had pumped Brandon for information, but he refused to talk even though he'd actually been a witness to the whole thing.

Brandon had slyly changed the subject, and they had ended up talking about their father, who had developed a mania about decorating the house for Christmas. Competitive decorating, Brandon had called it. Dad watched the decorations go up on other houses in the neighborhood, and he had an uncontrollable urge to put up decorations that were bigger, better, and more elaborate.

"I like Christmas," said Brenda to Kelly and Donna. "I really do. But my dad's gone positively jingle bells."

"How's that?" asked Donna.

"He's talking about motorized reindeer, and frozen artificial snowmen, and holograms of angels bobbing over a stable with real animals in it. I think he wants to rent Wise Men."

"Let me know if he finds any," Kelly said. "We'll run them for President." She and Donna laughed.

"This is serious," Brenda said. "He's made lists of special-effects houses and people who rent equipment to the movies. He's making drawings!"

"What does your mom say?" Donna asked.

"She's willing to see how far this goes." Brenda shook her head. "She thinks it's kind of cute, actually. Back in Minneapolis, Dad would put up the lights and help decorate the tree, and after that Christmas pretty much belonged to Mom."

"It's just a phase he's going through," Donna said.

"What does that mean?" Kelly asked.

"I don't know. That's what my mom always says about me when I do something she doesn't like."

"I wonder what sort of phase Steve is going through," Kelly said.

Here we go, Brenda thought. There was no way to avoid this topic.

Donna shook her head and said, "I can't believe Steve actually beat up Chuck Wilson."

Brenda gave in to the popular taste and asked, "What did they fight about, anyway?"

Wonderingly, Kelly said, "I told Steve that Chuck was taking me to the winter dance and he went ballistic. Talk about embarrassing. I can't believe he's being so immature."

Donna said dreamily, "Maybe someday someone will fight over me." She sighed.

Brenda tried to maintain a straight face. "I can just see it now: David Silver on a big white horse wielding a video camera." She looked at Kelly. Kelly looked at her. Together, they shook their heads and said, "Naw."

"If David Silver fought over me, he would do it for friendship," Donna said.

"Trust me, Donna," Kelly said. "Guys fighting over you is no big deal. It's just some macho thing, like seeing who has the shiniest car."

Brenda was pretty sure that competitive Christmas decorating was also some macho thing.

Brandon caught up with Steve outside Mr. Chapman's office. Steve stormed off and Brandon hurried after him. "So what happened?" Brandon asked.

"I'm suspended."

"What about Chuckie?"

Steve spun on Brandon and said, "Mr. Charles Wilson, esquire, will be attending school as usual." He marched across campus toward the student parking lot.

Steve was really angry, which Brandon could understand, but this whole situation had taken an ugly twist that had nothing to do with the fact that Steve was adopted. "Wait up, Steve," Brandon called after him. Steve didn't even slow down. "I don't get it," Brandon said as he trotted up even with Steve. "Why didn't he get suspended? Why just you?"

"Because *I* hit *him*," Steve said nastily.

"But he provoked you. It was just as much his fault as yours."

Steve stopped suddenly and looked at Brandon. In a tone that Brandon considered to be much too controlled for the gig, Steve said, "I know that, Brandon. Let's just say I'm a swell guy. Okay?"

"But you don't even like him," Brandon cried. Awful things were dammed up inside Steve. Brandon was sure of it.

"Long story. Look, Brandon, I appreciate your concern, but there's nothing you can do. I have to go." Steve didn't go. He looked toward the parking lot and tapped his foot.

"Maybe there is something I can do," Brandon said quietly. He pulled a minicassette tape from his pocket and said, "I have the whole event right here, Steve. All I have to do is play this for Mr. Chapman and he'll see why you swung at Chuckie."

"Please, Brandon. Stay out of this. Okay?" Steve squinted over Brandon's shoulder.

Brandon's entire body felt the frustration, the injustice of the situation, similar emotions to what Steve must be feeling. But more than that, Brandon felt confusion. Steve was not acting the way Steve should act under the circumstances. The need to get the story for the *Blaze* was long past, but the need to *get the story* remained. "But it's not fair," Brandon said even as he reflected that Steve must know this.

"Chuckie Wilson doesn't play fair. He never did."

Maybe an appeal to reason would help, though Brandon doubted it. "But if you're suspended, you can't take finals. You'll get an incomplete for the whole semester. Don't let the jerk get away with this. You have proof!" He shook the cassette in Steve's face.

Steve didn't flinch. He slapped Brandon once on the shoulder, advised him to hang loose, and strolled toward the student parking lot as if he hadn't a care in the world.

Brandon didn't get it. He was Steve's friend, and he wanted to do something about Steve's hurt. The fact that Steve wouldn't let him do that hurt Brandon, as well as confusing him.

Brandon tried to put all the pieces together as he walked slowly to the *Blaze* office. He ran over the situation again, ran over his conversation with Steve, and could make nothing more of it than he already had. Something was going on that Steve, for his own reasons, refused to share. Steve was a little hotheaded and self-centered, but he was no dummy. Maybe he was right: it was none of Brandon's business. Maybe it was none of anybody's business.

When he got to the *Blaze* office, he found John Griffin attempting to sell Andrea on an idea that disgusted Brandon. He settled on a stool in the corner and listened. Neither John nor Andrea took much notice of him.

"This fight is perfect for the story," John said with some eagerness. "If we only had a picture."

Andrea said, "I'm not the editor of some rag, John. This is the West Beverly *Blaze*. We've won national awards for journalism."

John shook his finger at Andrea and said, "I'm not going to let you go soft here, Zuckerman. This is the kind of thing the students of West Beverly High want to read about." He suddenly turned to Brandon and said, "You were there. What started the fight?"

"Give it a rest, John," Brandon said tiredly. If Steve thought it was none of his business, it was certainly none of John Griffin's, nor the student body's.

Kids passed outside the door. John looked accusingly over his shoulder at Andrea.

With uncertainty, Andrea said, "You *were* there, Brandon. Is the fight news?"

Brandon said, "No, Andrea, it's gossip. And I'm not interested."

John whirled on Andrea, and Brandon watched the expression on her face as he spoke. "If Brandon doesn't have the courage to write this story, I will. He wasn't the only witness. The public has a right to know."

To John's back, Brandon said, "Wrong. There is such a thing as a right to privacy, even for public figures, if that's what Chuckie Wilson is. Steve certainly isn't a public figure. Neither one of them is running for office. As far as I can tell, the public doesn't have any rights at all in this case. It's a private matter."

"Listen to him," John said. "He'll never make it on a college paper, let alone on a big city daily." John spoke with a contempt that sickened Brandon.

Brandon said, "I mean it, Andrea. I don't want to do this story, and I don't think anybody else should do it either." He pulled the notebook from his pocket and threw it onto Andrea's desk. "Here are my notes. Do what you think is best. Do what you think is right."

Andrea picked up the notebook but didn't look at it. Gently, she said, "Brandon, I. . . . What was the fight about?"

Brandon could not believe the effect John Griffin was having on Andrea. As far as Brandon was concerned, John was the guy who should have been suspended. Could you be suspended for muckraking?

"Andrea, if Steve wants to tell you what the fight was about, fine. But I'm not going to trash our friendship for a story," Brandon said.

Andrea appeared to be a little surprised at Brandon's outburst. That was okay with him. He couldn't stand to look at John or Andrea anymore. He couldn't stand to be in this room, this newspaper office anymore. He escaped into the hall and lost himself among the milling students.

Steve lay on his bed watching a tape of a "Hartley House" episode. He hated Chuckie. He hated "The Hartley House." And yet he felt compelled to watch it on TV, as a moth is compelled to dance closer and closer to the flame that will consume it if the moth gets too close. But Steve was no moth. He was looking for answers. He couldn't find them in his present life. Maybe he could find them in the sanitized middle-class morality of the show in which his mother had been so involved for so long.

Down the hall, his mom hummed the "Hartley House" theme as she got ready for a dinner meeting with her agent. The dinner was a big deal for her, but she and Steve hadn't had a chance to talk all afternoon, and Steve felt that it was necessary for them to talk now, before she left. He had some difficult stuff to unload, and he could contain it no longer.

Therefore, when she stood in his doorway,

pulling on first one pump and then the other, and chattering about Norman, and the steak she'd left in the freezer, and what time she'd be home, Steve stood up and said, "Mom, I need to talk to you."

"This isn't the best time, Gorgeous. It looks as if the whole reunion show may fall through. Chuck is wavering."

"Can we not talk about Chuckie and the reunion for one minute? I need you right now." It seemed to Steve that he was the only one trying to be reasonable. His mom asked him to act like an adult. Why couldn't she act like an adult for a change?

Sympathetically, Mrs. Sanders said, "I know I haven't been around much, Gorgeous, and I'm sorry. As soon as this is a done deal, we'll spend some quality time, just you and me. I promise."

Steve saw that he would have to bring up the big guns. He took a deep breath and said, "Mom, listen to me. I was suspended from school."

Steve was pleased to see that his announcement got a response from his mom. She seemed genuinely horrified. Maybe she wasn't entirely brain-dead yet.

She said, "What? You're telling me this now? Norman and all the junior agents are waiting for me at Enyart's for a major strategy session."

Maybe she *was* brain-dead. Or maybe just so far gone into show business la-la land that she couldn't see her way out anymore. Angry, hurt, and disgusted, Steve said, "I'm sorry my problems don't fit into your schedule."

"All right," Mrs. Sanders said. "Tell all." She sat on the end of Steve's bed and waited.

Steve retreated to his desk chair. Though he sincerely hated Chuckie Wilson, he felt bad about hitting him, not only for his mom's sake, but because it meant that Chuckie had succeeded in pushing Steve's buttons again. Steve hated having his buttons pushed at least as much as he hated Chuckie. Steve said, "I punched out Chuckie Wilson."

"Oh, my Lord," Mrs. Sanders said. For her, punching out Chuckie was obviously a bigger deal than being suspended from school. Steve's heart sunk. He didn't know what to feel anymore. As if to herself, Mrs. Sanders said, "Now I know why he's stalling on the reunion deal." She glared at Steve and said, "How could you do this to me?"

"To you?" Steve asked, too surprised to say more.

Mrs. Sanders stood and looked into the full-length mirror on Steve's bathroom door. She made minute adjustments to her costume while she spoke. "Fighting with my costar is not exactly going to get this show made, Steven. I thought I made myself very clear. I expected you to understand and cooperate. But you totally disregarded everything I said."

Defeated, Steve said, "I'm sorry, Mom, okay? I really am. But—"

"No buts. I was counting on you to help me. I *need* this job. You know that." She walked to the door.

"Fine. Go make your deals."

Steve spoke with such venom, that she turned to look at him, a little worry in her eyes. Steve said, "And by the way, don't worry about Chuckie. He'll do the show. I made sure of that." It was one of the few things he was sure of anymore. He needed advice and a sympathetic ear. If his mom was mentally in a different time zone, who would he talk to?

"What do you mean?" Mrs. Sanders asked.

"Ask Chuckie."

"Steve. Gorgeous. . . ." She foundered, not knowing what to say.

Steve said, "Good night, Mom. Have a nice meeting."

She smiled bleakly and went away.

Steve watched "Hartley House" episodes for hours. He could not help himself. Somewhere among all this artificially sweetened mess, there had to be a clue to Chuckie's vulnerability, to getting his mom's attention, to knowing what he should do with his life. The laugh track seemed to be having a good time, but Steve watched the show grimly, as if his personal tragedies were being played out on the TV screen.

Little five-year-old Chuckie was lying on the couch, bundled under blankets and cuddled with pillows. Mary Jo Hartley—as played by Samantha Sanders—shook down a thermometer and stuck it gently into Chuckie's mouth. "If you still have a fever, no school tomorrow." As she walked from the room, she said, "Now hold the thermometer under your tongue."

Around the thermometer, Chuckie said, "Okay, Mom."

As soon as Mary Jo was gone, the little dickens took the thermometer from his mouth and held it close to the light bulb in the table lamp. Big yocks from the audience.

Later, after it had been established that Chuckie really was sick, and didn't need to do the trick with the light bulb at all, Mary Jo read him the story of the Gingerbread Man, who was baked in the oven and then ran away.

When she'd finished the story, Chuckie asked, "Where did *I* come from, Mom?"

Mary Jo blanched, causing glee among the audience. She composed herself and said carefully, "Well, sweetheart, Daddy and I loved each other so much that one night there was so much love that it made a whole other person. And that person was you."

Chuckie was goggle-eyed by this story. He said, "That's not what Winfield Goulden says."

"Really?" Mary Jo said, bracing herself for Winfield Goulden's revelation.

"No. He showed me pictures at recess," Chuckie said.

"And where did Winfield say *he* came from?"

"Cleveland."

Big laugh from the audience. Steve, who was watching this wearily through half-closed eyes, could only shake his head.

Chuckie said, "So, where do *I* come from, Mom?"

Mary Jo swept Chuckie into a big hug. "Oh, Chuckie, you come from Philadelphia."

"Thanks, Mom."

"Chuckie, I love you."

Fade out. Insert commercial here.

By the time of the final hug and the final fade-out, Steve was still hopeful but no longer optimistic. He fell asleep with the most recent "Hartley House" tape still running. It whispered into his subconscious, and the words suggested an answer of sorts to Steve. Not an answer so much as a direction.

In his dream, Steve was still on his bed watching TV. Another Steve, his real age, was on TV sitting about where sick little Chuckie had been sitting. Mary Jo—or was it his mom? in the dream, the watching Steve was not sure—sat down on the couch and smiled her warmest, most motherly smile at him.

The TV Steve asked, "Where did *I* come from, Mom?"

"That's easy," said Mary Jo. "From Philadelphia."

The audience thought Mary Jo's answer was a scream. In that strange double-jointed way that dreams have, the watching Steve was able to look through the TV Steve's eyes, out to where the audience should have been. He saw only blackness. Where were the cameras and the lights? Where were the technicians? Their absence was curious, but it did not matter. What mattered at the moment was that the TV Steve had his mother's attention at last. The TV Steve said, "No, I mean, where did I really *come* from."

Mary Jo gave him a cute knowing smile and said, "I thought Winfield Goulden told you everything you needed to know at recess."

"I don't think I believed him."

Mary Jo spoke matter-of-factly, and without a hint of embarrassment. "Well, it's very simple, actually. An egg and a sperm get together to create a zygote which grows into a fetus."

"Yeah, but what about the love part?" asked the TV Steve with growing apprehension. "What about the part where you and Daddy loved each other so much that one night there was so much love that it made a whole other person? And that person was me."

The watching Steve was just as surprised as the TV Steve to see Chuckie, his high-school age, sitting on the arm of the couch behind Mary Jo. Chuckie said, "That's how they got me, Steve-o, not you."

The invisible audience laughed. Both Steves wondered who those brain-damaged guys were.

"Chuck's right, Gorgeous," Mary Jo said, "We went to the baby store for you." She turned and hugged Chuckie.

Over Mary Jo's shoulder, Chuckie said to the TV Steve, "Too bad you're adopted, Steve-o. But you must have a real mom somewhere."

Chuckie was right, the watching Steve decided. But so what?

The TV Steve looked straight out at the watching Steve and spoke to him. "Hey, man, you don't get it, do you?"

"Get what?" the watching Steve asked. The part of his brain that knew he was dreaming also knew this was very bizarre. He prepared himself to receive an important message from his subconscious.

The TV Steve said, "You're just an ornament around here, guy. Part of the set."

"But where did I come from?"

"If you want to know, go find your real parents."

This was a new idea for the watching Steve. He liked it but he still felt stupid. "But how? Where?"

"Oh," said the TV Steve offhandedly. "They're out there somewhere in television land. Right, Mary Jo?"

"Of course," said Mary Jo, very much in TV mom mode. "Everyone has a mother somewhere."

"Even in television land," said Chuckie. He laughed nastily.

The dream broke up after that. The TV Steve and the watching Steve—both dream Steves—coalesced into one and chased Chuckie through studio set after studio set, each more shadowy and bizarre than the last. After what seemed to be a very long time, Steve was alone on the set of the "Hartley House" living room with Chuckie's wild laughter echoing around him. The laughter faded, the light faded, and the real Steve slept fitfully for the rest of the night.

The next morning, Steve awoke knowing what he had to do but having no idea in the world how to begin. He showered, dressed, and went downstairs to make a pot of coffee. He poured a cup and hunched over it at the breakfast bar. As he sipped coffee, his resolve hardened. But where to begin? Where to begin?

Mrs. Sanders blew into the kitchen like a tornado of pixie dust. "Good morning, Gorgeous," she cried happily. "Good morning. Good morning."

Steve grunted. He was still angry from the previous night. Slack was not a thing he was prepared to give anybody, least of all his mom. Correction: least of all, Mrs. Sanders, the insensitive lady with whom he lived in this house.

Mrs. Sanders took an egg from the refrigerator, laughed at her own foolishness, and put it back. "No eggs for me, thank you. Today I start my diet. The camera puts on ten pounds and I want to be ready for it." She poured herself a cup of coffee and settled with it next to Steve. Steve pretended to take no notice.

Her gaiety became forced. She said, "Today is one of those good days, the kind you want to remember and enjoy."

Steve still didn't give her anything. He supposed that she'd finally made the "Hartley House" deal. That was fine. At least his suspension had paid off. But he had more important things to worry about, and this woman would not be part of them.

"Come on, Gorgeous. Let me see one of those million-dollar smiles."

"I don't have anything to smile about."

"You will."

Steve glanced at her with a sarcastic curl of his lip.

"Come on, Gorgeous. I have a surprise for you."

Despite himself, Steve said, "What?"

"If I tell you, it won't be a surprise. Come on."

Mrs. Sanders took him by the hand and led him outside. In the driveway was a new red Stingray with an enormous white bow on top.

"What's this?" Steve asked. He thought he knew but he didn't want to be correct.

"It's your new car, silly. If you can't bend your face into a grin, how about a plain old-fashioned, 'thanks, Mom.'"

The Stingray was a boss piece of machinery, all right, but Steve had the suspicion that he was being purchased, as surely as the car had been purchased. He did not like the feeling. Before he got excited, he wanted to make sure. "What's all this about?"

Mrs. Sanders buffed a spot on the fender with her sleeve, and said, "You were right. Chuck finally agreed to do the reunion show, and he said that you had something to do with it. So . . ." She indicated the car with one hand, as if she were doing a commercial. "Thanks, Gorgeous."

There it was. The worst possible reason Mrs.

Sanders could have chosen for buying him a car. He did not believe it was possible for him to be more disgusted than he'd felt the night before, but here was this situation, making him wrong. He said, "I don't believe what I'm hearing. But then, sensitivity was never your strong suit."

"What?" Mrs. Sanders asked, puzzled.

Mrs. Sanders's innocence inflamed Steve, and he could no longer hold in the thing that angered and hurt him the most. He said, "If you'd been as sensitive as Mary Jo Hartley, you might have told me I was adopted before you broadcast it to Chuckie and half the known universe."

"What are you talking about?"

"You didn't tell me I was adopted till I was sixteen years old. Chuckie says he's known since we were seven. He says everybody knew."

"I didn't tell him, Steve."

For a moment, Steve wondered if Chuckie had lied to him just to cause this very kind of scene. After all, Chuckie had never been anything but unpleasant, whereas this Mrs. Sanders person had always acted like, well, like a mom. "If you didn't tell him, then who did?"

"I don't know. I swear I don't know."

She walked to Steve and reached out to him, but he backed away. As far as he was concerned, her answer was not convincing. Though his mind was in turmoil, Steve was thinking clearly enough to know that the information could have come only from Mrs. Sanders. Taking that along with the abuse he'd been taking from Chuckie, and the lack of sympathy he'd been getting from her, he was ready to believe the worst. "At least now I know why I've always felt like a second-class citizen around that creep."

"He's not that bad, really."

This woman still didn't get it. Was she an idiot or just so focused on her career that nothing else mattered? Still he could not let her go. He had too much emotion invested over too many years. Steve said, "Are you listening to me here? Chuckie is that bad. He is! Do you know why I was suspended? He said he wouldn't do your lousy show unless I took the rap for the fight." He slapped the sun-warmed hood of the car, startling both of them. "And this is my commission."

Mrs. Sanders rubbed one eye with the heel of her hand. "Steve, Gorgeous, that's not true."

"It is true." Steve was rolling now. His emotional inertia would not allow him to stop, would not allow him to think before he said things he would regret later. He was damned angry, and regret—while considered—was disregarded as a weak thing of no importance. "Maybe you adopted me because you thought motherhood was some kind of role you could play. You could put it on and take it off with your makeup. Well, it isn't. It's real."

Mrs. Sanders wrung her hands. "Steve, Steve—"

"And that's why I'm going to find my real parents." Having said this, Steve felt momentary relief, as if he'd coughed up a lump that had been blocking his throat.

"Oh, my Lord," said Mrs. Sanders. "That's what this is all about?"

"You got that right," Steve said, and he marched toward the house. He had bags to pack, plans to make, people to see.

"Steve, please," Mrs. Sanders said as she grabbed him by the arm.

He shrugged her off and kept moving. "Leave me alone."

She called to him, "I know I wasn't a perfect mother, but I did the best I could. I love you, Steve. For heaven's sake, I chose you."

Steve walked into the house and leaned briefly on the breakfast bar. The top was cool against the hot skin of his forearms. In his stomach, where the writhing snakes had been, was a great emptiness. He didn't know who he was. And the fact that he'd hurt that woman outside terribly did not make him feel any better, though she had hurt him first, and he felt justified. But he had to fill the emptiness, and the only way he could do that was by discovering the truth about himself.

He suspected that the truth, whatever it was, would not be as simple as the naive school-yard pronouncements of Winfield Goulden. And the word "Philadelphia" would not even begin to describe it.

5

The need to know

IN SCHOOL THE NEXT DAY, TALK ABOUT THE
fight between Chuck and Steve was dying down, and
talk about the winter dance gradually made a come-
back. As they walked through the halls between
classes, Brandon shook his head while Brenda tried
to convince him that going to the dance would not
ruin his standing as a wallflower and as an all-around
man of mysterious virtue. Brandon contemplated
how different twins could be.

"But I dance like a white guy," he said.

"You don't actually have to dance. I know you
can drink punch. I've seen you."

"Just my luck Andrea would show up and
make me minuet or something."

"If you tried to minuet to Guns N' Roses, you'd break a leg."

"See, Bren? This dancing stuff can be dangerous." Hoping to avoid further argument, he called, "How you doing, dudes and dudettes?" and pulled Brenda into a group consisting of Kelly, Chuck Wilson, and Dylan. Chuck's eye was a little swollen, and the area around it was a blot of interesting colors. Brandon didn't like to hang around with the guy, but at the moment it was unavoidable.

Dylan grabbed Brenda, and she gave him a smooch on the cheek. Good, Brandon thought. Brenda's been distracted from thinking about the dance.

"What's so interesting?" Brandon asked. He looked where everybody else was looking, and saw Donna talking to David Silver at the far end of the hall. If body language meant anything, they were really stoked on each other.

"I don't know what Donna sees in him," Kelly said.

"Come on, Kel," Dylan said. "David's a good kid."

"Good and young, you mean," Brenda said. "He's not even sixteen."

Chuck had draped himself around Kelly, and she was trying to act as if she were comfortable. Knowing what he knew about Chuck, Brandon was definitely not comfortable. Chuck said, "Older women/younger guy couples are big. Look at Cher."

"Looking's a start, I guess," Dylan said dreamily. Brenda punched him in the shoulder.

With a last fond glance, David walked away from Donna, and she joined them.

"So, Donna," Dylan said, "are you sure your reputation can stand the stigma of going out with a younger guy?"

Donna tried to be reasonable, but when she spoke, she could not hide a sharp edge of anger. Brandon knew she'd been hassled about David Silver a lot lately. She said, "I'm not going out with him, Dylan. I'm just giving him a ride to the dance."

They all watched her, waiting for more.

"So his father doesn't have to drive him."

Kelly grinned and said, "You better be careful, Donna. David is jailbait."

"Would you guys cut it out? David and I are just friends. As in platonic friends. So stop already."

Brandon decided that now was the time to do Donna and himself a favor by breaking up this group. He said, "Uh, Kelly, can I talk to you for a minute?"

"What's up, Brandon?"

Brandon was aware that everybody was looking at him. Having secrets was okay. But announcing to the group at large that you were about to share a secret with only part of the group was not good manners. Brandon didn't see any way around it. "Can we talk alone?"

"Sure." She patted Chuckie on the cheek, and said, "I'll be right back."

"That's okay," said Chuckie. "I have a meeting at the studio. See you tonight. Hang loose, dudes."

As Chuckie moved out of earshot, Brenda said, "He is *so* adorable."

"I heard that," Dylan said.

"Come on," Brandon said to Kelly.

They strolled down the hall trying to avoid the worst knots of kids. Brandon was glad to have the few minutes to gather his thoughts. He knew that he was doing the right thing, yet he could not help suspecting that he was mixing in where he didn't belong. If Steve wanted Kelly to know something, he'd tell her, wouldn't he? Maybe not. Maybe he didn't want to burden her with his problems. Maybe he didn't want her to know how much power little Chuckie had over his life. Where Kelly was concerned, it was hard to know what Steve would do.

They reached a place of relative quiet near a case full of ancient team photographs and dusty football trophies. Brandon said, "Kelly, I don't mean to step on you, but I can't believe you're still going to the dance with that loser after what went down between him and Steve."

Amazed, Kelly asked, "That's what you needed to talk to me about?"

"You need to know the truth, Kelly. I was there."

"I didn't have to be there to know what happened. Steve's jealous, that's all. He punched Chuck out because he doesn't want Chuck taking me to the dance."

Brandon sliced the air with a hand and said, "Wrong, Kelly. You had nothing to do with it."

Kelly hesitated for a moment before she asked, "What do you mean?"

"You know how sensitive Steve is about being adopted."

"Sure."

"Chuckie knows, too. And he was giving Steve a major hard time about it."

Brandon had watched Kelly's expression change from sarcasm and disgust to doubt to genuine concern. She said, "Oh, no. Poor Steve."

"Poor Steve doesn't even begin to cover the wringer Chuckie has put him through. He hates Chuckie, and from what I've seen, Steve has good reason."

"What do you want me to do?"

"Just think about it. That's all."

Kelly frowned.

"Just think about it." Brandon walked away. He had confidence in her. She and Steve had had their ups and downs over the years, but Brandon suspected that she harbored a fondness for him that had nothing to do with who was dating whom. On the other hand, maybe she was just a human being who didn't like to see one person stick pins in another.

■ ■ ■

Steve waited until the school day began, and then he drove to the Walsh house. He needed advice from somebody normal. And the most normal person he could think of was Cindy Walsh, Brenda and Brandon's mom. He lifted his finger to the doorbell button and let his hand drop without ringing.

Steve did not feel the hot anger and frustration that had driven him earlier. But the emptiness remained and had taken over. Mrs. Sanders didn't matter anymore. She'd probably done the best she could with the entire "Hartley House" situation, and the car was just a mistake. Anybody could make a mistake. If Steve held anything against her, it was her blindness to what a jerk Chuckie Wilson was and had been for years.

And Steve felt that he had been a wuss for taking what Chuckie had been handing him. Of course, when he'd stopped taking it, when he'd punched out Chuckie's lights, he'd been suspended for his trouble. He couldn't win. Only Chuckie continued to win. Chuckie held all the big cards.

And now this new business about needing to know who his real parents were. The question had taken him by the throat and would not release him. He shrugged. He had to have some answers. That's why he was here. He rang the doorbell.

The front door opened and Cindy Walsh

peered out at him with surprise. She smiled and said, "Well hello, Steve. You just missed Brenda and Brandon."

"I figured that." Why did this have to be so difficult? It would be easy to just say, "Thanks," and walk away. Mrs. Walsh would think his behavior odd, but not significant. But if he just went home, he'd never find out anything. Besides that, if he went home now he'd feel like a fool. He said, "Can I come in?"

"Shouldn't you be in school?" Mrs. Walsh asked gently.

"Didn't they tell you? I was suspended."

"Oh. Well, of course. Come on in." She opened the door wider.

Steve sensed her watching him, trying to figure him out as he walked to the kitchen. He sat down at the kitchen table. Early American. A big bowl of fruit in the middle. Real fruit, not wax or plastic. Very nice. Very normal. Steve folded his hands before him. He was more nervous than he would be if he was going to take a test.

Mrs. Walsh took up a position leaning against the sink and asked, "Can I fix you some breakfast, Steve?"

"No thanks. I already ate." He looked around the bright friendly kitchen trying to find something to say. Normally, he had no trouble speaking with parents or with anybody else. He was a glib guy—too glib, some said. A silver-tongued devil. But it was not often that he revealed so much of himself as he was about to reveal to

Cindy Walsh. He wanted to trust her, knew he could trust her, and yet opening up was hard. He was out of practice because he hated to be vulnerable. He said, "I sort of have nothing to do."

"I see," Mrs. Walsh said and smiled. If she could flash that thing on demand, she could make a million bucks as a TV mom. "Well, I'm flattered you decided to do it with me."

"No big deal." Steve looked at his hands and said, "I didn't come over just to take up your time and space, Mrs. Walsh. I had a reason."

"Really?"

He might as well be tearing off pieces of himself. With difficulty, he said, "Mrs. Walsh, you're a mother."

Mrs. Walsh seemed surprised at Steve's statement. "I sure am," she said with pride.

"Well, I was wondering: If Brenda and Brandon were adopted, I mean, hypothetically speaking, if they were adopted, what would you think if they came to you and told you they wanted to find their natural parents?"

Mrs. Walsh seemed a little confused by his long rambling question. "What do you mean?"

Steve tried again, this time asking the question he really wanted answered. He asked, "How would you feel?"

Mrs. Walsh contemplated him for a moment, and then asked, "Steve, what prompts the sudden interest in this subject?"

Steve said the first thing that came into his

head, and then realized how ridiculous it sounded. "School paper. I'm taking a poll." Why would
somebody who'd been suspended be taking a poll
for the school paper? He attempted to compose
his face into a neutral expression, and went on, "I
really would like to know. I mean, would you be
mad? Would you be hurt?"

Mrs. Walsh wrestled with his question. He'd
come to the right place. He would get a straight
answer from her.

She said, "Well, I don't think I'd be mad.
Maybe a little. But I suppose that more than any
thing else, I'd be afraid."

"Why afraid?"

"I'd be afraid that if my children found their
natural mother I might lose them."

He thought of Mrs. Sanders's reaction that
morning, when he'd announced that he wanted to
find his natural mother. But neither Mrs. Sanders
nor Mrs. Walsh recognized the strength of his
need, that he'd never wanted anything so much in
his life. He said, "But wouldn't you understand
that they had to know, that they had to find out
where they really came from?"

"I would, Steve. If I could. But emotions are
funny things. Sometimes they blind you to the
most obvious ideas."

She looked him right in the eyes, her face a
mask of motherly compassion. She knew what he
was, Steve was certain of it, and he hoped it
wouldn't matter.

Mrs. Walsh said, "Have you thought about this, Steve? What if a child's natural parents don't want to be found? I mean, nobody gives up a child without a good reason."

"I guess a kid in this position would have to take that risk." He couldn't sit here anymore. He had to get moving, to start the investigation. Besides, pretty soon Mrs. Walsh would dig deeper, and they would both end up crying. Steve didn't want to cry here in the Walsh kitchen. He had the feeling that there would be plenty of time for tears later. "Well, I better go," he said as he headed for the kitchen door.

Mrs. Walsh said, "Steve?"

"Yeah?"

"Good luck."

Embarrassed by her concern, he ducked his head and left as quickly as he could. He drove away not really knowing where he would go. He wasn't ready to go home and face Mrs. Sanders just yet. He had a lot of things to think about, a lot of things to straighten out before he did that.

6

Life's little mysteries

MECHANICALLY, STEVE WENT THROUGH the motions of driving and found himself going north on Pacific Coast Highway. It was a beautiful day, not a bad day to be suspended. The ocean sparkled and had deeper blue places above which gulls wheeled and called to each other. The wind blew cold and salty against his face, and brought the green and slightly fishy smell of seaweed.

He advised himself to relax, to hang loose, to allow his subconscious—which had gotten him into this mess—to come up with a solution.

He tried to sort his feelings about Mrs. Sanders. Except for lately, during this regrettable Chuckie Period, he and she got along pretty well.

Did he want to throw his entire life away? Maybe they could just be friends. That would be great.

The big question was, could he be friends with his real mom? After all, she'd given him away. They were really strangers. In Steve's head, the features on his real mom's face kept drifting around until it looked like the face of Samantha Sanders. This disturbed Steve. Samantha Sanders was a nice lady who had taken care of him, not his real mom.

For a moment Steve frightened himself with the notion that his real mom wouldn't even want to talk to him, and that Samantha Sanders wouldn't take him back. He'd be some kind of bizarre orphan. He'd probably end up living in his car. Until he had to sell it for food. Well, he'd told Mrs. Walsh that a kid in his position had to take risks. This was just another risk.

Steve drove almost as far north as Santa Barbara before he turned back, still without an answer in his head. The only decision he made was that he would be polite but firm with Samantha Sanders. He loved her. Even at the worst moments, he never questioned that. But he still had to know who his real mom was. Mrs. Sanders would have to trust him to come back, the way Mrs. Walsh would.

By the time he got back to Beverly Hills, the school day was almost over. He still put off going home. The confrontation with Mrs. Sanders would be hideous.

During school, the Peach Pit would be nearly deserted, and would be the perfect place to sit and work up his courage. Nat probably wouldn't bother him as long as he kept buying coffee.

He walked into the warm quiet room. It smelled of grease and sugar and fruit pies. Golden afternoon light slanted through the blinds onto the floor in parallel lines. A burly guy, probably the owner of the truck out back, was engulfing a hamburger.

Nat came out from the kitchen and was surprised to see Steve. Nat was a short, blocky man with the well-used face of a friendly head of cauliflower. He was wiping his hands on his apron, on brown smudges where he'd obviously wiped them before.

"Can I get a burger and some rings?" Steve asked.

"I think that can be arranged." He peered at Steve as if trying to read words on his face. "You got a lot of color for a guy who spent the day in school."

"Long story." Nat was a friendly guy, and he would probably be compassionate, but Steve did not consider him a close friend, not even as close as Mrs. Walsh. All they generally talked about was college basketball.

Nat shrugged and said, "Must be. You don't look so hot. Everything okay?"

"I'm fine."

Nat pondered Steve for a moment longer, then

nodded and went back into the kitchen, where he threw a hamburger patty on the grill and plunged a cup of onion rings into the hot grease. Everything began to hiss.

Steve spoke to him through the window. "Tell me something, Nat. Who do you look like, your mother or your father?"

After a moment of consideration, Nat said, "My mother, I guess. She's gone now, but everyone always used to say we had the same face. What about you?"

"I don't know. That's the trouble." He spoke as if the admission didn't mean much. As if it were just another one of life's little mysteries.

Behind Steve, the door opened and Nat said hello to Dylan. Dylan sat down next to Steve at the counter and said, "Hey, bro. How's it going?"

Steve glanced at his watch. After three. School was out. In another fifteen minutes, the Peach Pit would be a zoo. It was time to move along. But Steve had ordered food, and he felt obligated to stay.

From the kitchen, Nat called, "Cheer this kid up, Dylan. Even the prospect of a burger and rings don't lift his spirits."

Steve was aware that Dylan was staring at him. Before Steve could decide whether to explain what was going on, Dylan demanded, "Talk."

"Well, if anyone would understand, you would, I guess." Dylan knew where his parents were, but they might as well have been treasures with just *X*s to mark their locations. His mom was some flake doing crystal therapy and spiritual massage in Hawaii, and his dad was in jail for some stock fraud nobody but an accountant would understand.

"I'm listening," Dylan said.

Nat brought the burger and rings, and hung around for a moment as if he wanted to be included in the conversation. When he saw that all Steve was going to do was eat, he moved away and took the order of some kids who were sitting in a booth in the back.

Steve lowered his voice and said, "I never told you this, but I'm adopted." It was hard to get the words out, like squeezing the last bit of toothpaste out of the tube.

"Wow," said Dylan and apparently meant it.

With this encouragement, Steve explained, "For my whole life, I thought I was Samantha Sanders's son. And then, suddenly, I wasn't." He put down the burger. It tasted funny, but he was sure the burger was not at fault. Just thinking about being adopted seemed to change his entire body, make it need and feel different things, as if he'd gotten it at a department story instead of growing it himself.

"And now?" Dylan asked.

"I want to find my real parents. I want to know who they are, where they're from, why they gave me up."

"Are you sure you want to do this?"

"I have to." Steve had already thought about the question too much not to know the answer.

"OK. But just because some lady out there is your mother doesn't mean you're going to have an instant relationship. I've been there."

"I know." Steve had seen Dylan attempt getting along with his mom. It was pretty ugly.

"Listen: Samantha Sanders may not have given birth to you, but she was there for you. Doesn't that count for something?"

Steve brooded about Dylan's question. Sure, Samantha Sanders got points for being there, big points. But that didn't prevent Steve from being curious about his secret origins. He and Dylan were talking about two separate things.

Andrea Zuckerman descended onto the stool on Steve's other side. "Hey, guys," she said. Steve hated it when she was chipper. She glanced at Dylan, made a decision, and said, "Steve, I've been looking for you. I was talking to Brandon. I need to ask you something."

Andrea! Steve thought excitedly. He said, "Yeah? I want to ask you a question, too." He should have thought of Andrea before, what with her public service activities and interest in weird causes, she was the perfect person to talk to about his problem.

"Okay. You go first," Andrea said.

"When you were at Rapline, did you ever talk to any adopted kids who wanted to find their real parents?"

"Sure. Why?"

"I have this friend, see . . ." He stopped. It sounded bogus, even to him.

But Andrea seemed willing to go along with the gag. She nodded and said, "Okay."

"No. I don't have a friend. I'm the one who's adopted."

"Heavy," Andrea said. "I had no idea. You look so much like your mom."

"That's what I was thinking, too," Dylan said.

Steve shrugged. He didn't like the direction this conversation was taking. He said, "Yeah, well, maybe adopted kids are like puppies. They grow up to look like their owners."

Andrea smiled at that and then got serious. She said, "Are you sure you want to do this?"

Why did everybody question his decision? Couldn't they see how important this was? "I need to know where I come from. Tell me where to start."

Andrea frowned as she thought. Steve took another bite of his burger. It wasn't so bad, really, having a department store body.

"From what I hear," Andrea said, "finding natural parents is a tough thing to do. Sometimes it's impossible."

"There must be records."

"Always. But sometimes the natural parents have them sealed so some kid can't do exactly what you're trying to do."

Steve chewed glumly. Scratched before he

even started. It wasn't like he wanted anything from them—just to say hello, to find out some things. He didn't want money, or even very much time. Tears came, but he fought them back.

Andrea said, "But the news isn't all bad. Organizations exist that help adopted kids. You could start there. But you need some clues, guy. You need a place to start or the process could take years."

"I'll live with it. What did you want to ask me?"

Suddenly, Andrea became flustered. She said, "Nothing," and laughed insincerely.

Andrea's problems didn't concern Steve at the moment. He had enough of his own. For one thing, he wondered where he could hire a good private detective. Andrea fidgeted next to him the entire time he ate his burger. He and Dylan talked about the possibility of skiing together during Christmas break. It was a pleasure to not speak about his problems for a moment.

When he was done, Andrea had finally justified a piece of peach pie to herself and was vacillating over whether she should have it with ice cream. Steve left money on the counter and drove home trying not to think about anything.

His mom's car was there, so she was probably inside. He had to speak with her some time. He owed her that at least. Besides, if Andrea was right, he needed to ask her a few questions, or he *would* be spending years on his project, a prospect that did not appeal to him.

He opened the front door, and she called to him from the living room. "Hello, Gorgeous."

He found her standing in front of the couch with a wrinkled handkerchief in her hand. Her eyes were red, as if she'd been crying. She smiled at him and held out her arms. And though a hug was definitely out of the question, Steve could not find it in himself to be rude.

"Shouldn't you be at the studio?" he asked in the friendliest tone he could manage.

"I'm not going to do the show, Steve."

Steve goggled at her and said, "What?"

"For an agent, Norman is pretty sentimental. He decided that the perfect place to sign the deal memo would be the sound stage where we used to do 'The Hartley House.'" She looked at her hands and tore a shred of tissue into smaller pieces. "Norman and Chuckie were already there. I heard them talking, but I couldn't see them because some flats were in the way."

Steve listened to Mrs. Sanders, fascinated but numb. The story she told did not concern him, yet it was the most interesting story in the world.

Mrs. Sanders said, "Norman was promising that Chuckie would be the next Michael J. Fox, and Chuckie was believing him."

"Right in character for both of them," Steve said.

Mrs. Sanders smiled and went on. "They were standing under a work light next to a battered table that had a bottle and three paper cups on it.

Norman and Chuckie and I were going to toast our show with apple juice. I told them that you should have been there, too. After all, you were the one who got Chuckie to do the show."

"Yeah," Steve said with disgust. "I'll bet they loved to hear that."

Chuckie lifted his paper cup and said, "You're right, Mom. To Steve."

The three of them drank, and then Mrs. Sanders asked innocently, "What exactly did he say that was so convincing?"

Chuckie shrugged, and seemed to suffer a momentary discomfort. "Oh, nothing specific."

"Steve's a great kid, Samantha," Norman said.

Mrs. Sanders shook her head. "What happened between you two, anyway? You know how I hate to see you fight."

"Oh, you know Steve. Mister Sensitive." Chuckie grinned and sipped his apple juice."

"He is. About some things," Mrs. Sanders admitted. "So. Charles. Tell me, how did you know he was adopted?"

Chuckie and Norman shifted their eyes at each other. Chuckie said, "Everybody knew, didn't they?"

Lightly, Mrs. Sanders said, "As a matter of fact, everybody did not know."

Norman quickly explained, "I told him, Sam. Okay?" He made an offhanded gesture. "But that was all a long time ago. We have more important things to think about now. Like the show. Like how we're going to spend all the money. More apple juice?" He lifted the bottle.

Mrs. Sanders asked, "You told him, Norman? Why?" She was apparently just making conversation.

Evidently, Norman did not entirely buy Mrs. Sanders's casual attitude. Cagily, he explained, "You know how the two of them were always fighting. They were just little boys. One day, Chuck was jealous of Steve. I thought telling him might make Chuck feel better."

Mrs. Sanders's face became red and curled into a snarl. She set down her cup hard enough to slosh apple juice onto the ancient table. "You betrayed my trust so you could make a spoiled brat feel better?" Her tone spoke of anger and utter disbelief.

Chuckie dropped all pretense of politeness. He pointed a finger at Mrs. Sanders and said, "Hey, lady, it was this spoiled brat who kept you on the air. And don't forget why I'm doing this reunion show. I know how important it is to you."

"Not as important as my son."

"Sam, please," Norman said. He lifted his open hands and tried to calm her. "This is all a misunderstanding."

"On the contrary, Norman. I believe that I understand at last. One of the things I understand is that I've put up with the hired garbage for too long. Good-bye, Norman. Have a nice career, Chuckie."

■   ■   ■

"You just walked out?" Steve asked, amazed.

"I did." She stepped forward to hug him, and Steve did not back away.

Weasels danced in Steve's head and in his stomach. They were no great improvement over the snakes, only more energetic. One weasel implored Steve to give up his search for his real parents. The other, while sympathetic to Mrs. Sanders's feelings and to the depth of her sacrifice, could not shake his curiosity about Steve's origins.

While she and Steve hugged, Mrs. Sanders said, "All those years I forced you to be nice to that half-pint bastard. I promise you, Steve, you will never have to be nice to him again."

This was wonderful. This was awful. Steve didn't know what to do. He knew only two things. One was that having asked the question, he still needed to know the answer. He spoke the other thing he knew: "I love you, Mom." He began to ball like a kid. He let himself go and just did it.

"I love you, too, baby," Mrs. Sanders said, and hugged Steve even harder.

They both got fresh tissues and laughed as they dabbed their eyes and blew their noses.

"I know this is hard, Mom, but I need to know. Where did I come from? And don't say Philadelphia."

"Why would I say . . . ?" And then she seemed

to remember the episode Steve had seen on tape that morning.

"My mother. Who was my real mother?"

Mrs. Sanders sank to the couch and began to shred her tissue again. Steve hated to see her like this, but she was the only person who had the answers he needed.

Almost to herself, Mrs. Sanders said, "I've been dreading this moment for seventeen years. That's why I waited so long to tell you the truth." She looked up at him pleadingly. "I'm scared, Steve."

"I know," Steve said and sat down next to her.

"I just don't want to lose you."

Steve took her hand and patted it while he tried to think of something comforting to say.

7

The last dance

STEVE AND HIS MOTHER—THE PINCH-mother who had raised him with love and understanding, not the mystery woman who'd shipped him off to parts unknown—sat on the couch for a long time. Tears dried and they continued to sit. They spoke of Christmases past and of the Christmas that was yet to be in less than a month. For the sake of the present, Steve allowed his questions about the past to slide, at least for the moment. He still needed to know.

The doorbell rang and Steve went to answer it. Outside was a man with their Christmas tree. For a few minutes, Steve lost himself in the small prosaic details of getting the tree into the house, of setting it up straight in exactly the right place. He and his mom worked as a team, directing the delivery man, laughing with the pleasure of it all.

After the delivery man left, Steve and his mom got out box after box of Christmas fantasy, ornaments that had been passed down through the family for years, others that had come with burgers at the local chain outlet the year before.

For a long time, they just looked at the empty tree. Trees without decking looked all right in the wild, Steve thought, surrounded by dirt and sky and other trees, but without an excuse for being there, without its Christmas colors, a tree inside a house looked slightly ridiculous. Mrs. Sanders tore a few needles from the tree, crushed them between her fingers and smelled them. She smiled and held the crushed needles out to Steve. He inhaled the pine scent, still a happy surprise after all these years.

However, Christmas was not the subject uppermost in Steve's mind. He said, "I don't want to hurt you, but this is something I have to do."

Mrs. Sanders sank to the floor of the foyer, and for a moment Steve thought she was going to cry again; but she only began to open the boxes of tree decorations. There were colored globes, Santas and reindeer—one Santa turning the crank on a red and green movie camera, wires of lights. She looked at the ornaments as she said, "I know." She sighed. "Your mother's name is Karen Brown."

Steve repeated the simple words as if they were a magic charm. The weasels rested. The snakes had gone away.

"She came from a small town somewhere outside Albuquerque. That's where you were born."

"Wow," Steve said with quiet amazement, so overcome he was afraid that speaking too loud would break the spell and he would turn out not to have a real mother after all. "My mother's name is Karen. Karen Brown. I was born in Albuquerque. Wow." Steve was fascinated by the sound of his mother's name, by the name of a city that till this moment had meant nothing. He felt like the man who was delighted to discover that all his life he'd been speaking prose.

Mrs. Sanders said, "I wish I could tell you more. All I know is that she was very young." She looked up at Steve and smiled beatifically, like a madonna, with pleasure, acceptance, and forgiveness. "She must have been very beautiful."

Steve dropped to his knees next to Mrs. Sanders and touched a red globe. He said, "I have to go."

"Go where?" She spoke with some fear, as if she already knew.

"To Albuquerque. I have to find her, Mom."

Mrs. Sanders bit her lip and nodded.

"I have to go now. Tonight."

"Tonight? But it's almost Christmas. We've been together every Christmas for your whole life. Look: we haven't even decorated the tree."

Steve took her hand between both of his. "I'm

sorry, Mom. I know. But this year . . ." He shook his head. There were too many decisions to make. Too much pain. "I'm sorry."

Mrs. Sanders nodded. Her eyes were wet, as were Steve's, but neither of them sobbed. She said, "Just do one thing for me before you go." She handed him a white cardboard box big enough for a single shoe. Inside was an angel made of white feathers. "You insisted that putting on the angel was your job. I used to have to lift you so you could reach the top of the tree."

Steve gently took the angel from the box, and reached to settle it on the tree's spire. He no longer needed his mom's help, but if she had not been there for him in times past, he would not be here now. "Merry Christmas, Mom," he said.

They both looked up at the angel, alone at the top of the tree. The doorbell rang, startling everyone but the angel.

"Kelly," Steve said with surprise. "I thought you were going to the dance with Chuckie." It was amazing. He could say the little creep's name now without getting angry. Chuckie was just a creep, no longer his personal demon.

Kelly looked foxy in a shiny green party dress. A sprinkle of red glitter was in her hair. She shrugged and said, "When I heard what he did to you, I decided that standing him up was the best way to get even."

Steve really did love this woman. If only they could get along.

Together forever. Shannen Doherty as Brenda Walsh and
Luke Perry as Dylan McKay.

Pretty in pink. Jennie Garth as Kelly Taylor.

Starry-eyed Shannen Doherty as Brenda Walsh.

Tori Spelling as
fashionable
Donna Martin.

Brian Austin Green as
romantic David Silver.

Ian Ziering as "tough guy with a heart" Steve Sanders.

Gabrielle Carteris as brainy but beautiful Andrea Zuckerman.

Jason Priestley as Brandon Walsh.

Luke Perry as Dylan McKay.

Dashing duo. Ian Ziering as Steve Sanders and Brian Austin Green as David Silver.

"It's a nice night. Want to go for a ride?" She smiled apprehensively, as if afraid he'd turn her down.

Steve felt a little nervous himself, as if this were a first date, which in a funny way, it was. By Kelly's standing up Chuckie, by her coming here, by Steve's feeling a new warmth toward her, they had reached a new level of intimacy. Oh, Kelly was still a knock-out, but at the moment her physical beauty mattered less than the fact that she was one terrific human being.

"Yes, I would," Steve said. "But give me a minute to throw a few things together."

"What things? We're just going for a drive." Kelly studied him with sudden suspicion. "Aren't we?" She looked at Mrs. Sanders over Steve's shoulder.

Mrs. Sanders shook her head and ran upstairs.

"What's going on?" Kelly asked.

"You're one of the few people who knew I was adopted."

"Well, yeah, but—"

"I'm going to Albuquerque to find my real mom, a lady named Karen Brown. I'm going tonight if I can."

"Tonight?" Kelly seemed to be as astonished as Samantha Sanders had been.

Steve smiled and shrugged. "I have to go before I lose my nerve." He took a few steps toward the stairs. "Wait here. Give me time to get a few things and to call the bus station."

"Bus station?" Kelly asked with disbelief.

Steve's decision to take the bus had come out of nowhere, but now that he'd said it, he knew that taking the bus was the only way for him to get to Albuquerque. He stopped on the bottom step and said, "Look, Kel, I'm going to Boondocks, New Mexico, to dig up my roots. I think I ought to leave Beverly Hills behind."

"But why a bus? You could fly."

"I could, but I think that taking a bus is the least Beverly Hills thing I can think of; it's about right for this gig. Besides, taking the bus will give me more time to think."

Kelly nodded.

Steve went upstairs and collected shirts, pants, underwear, and a secret stash of cash he had been keeping for emergencies. Then, with his full overnight bag next to him on the bed, he called the bus station. The next bus to Albuquerque and points east would leave at 11:59 that night. According to the guy, there were always a few empty seats. A ticket was surprisingly cheap.

Steve carried his bag down the hall to where his mom sat on the edge of her bed looking at a framed photo of the two of them together.

"I'm going," Steve said, almost wishing that he weren't.

"Good luck," Mrs. Sanders said.

"Thanks. Uh, merry Christmas."

"Merry Christmas, Steve." She smiled at him.

He gave a small casual wave and walked away.

It was either that or spend more hours crying and talking.

"Let's go," Steve said, and hurried past Kelly, who still stood in the open front doorway. He walked to her BMW, turned, and saw her pull the front door shut.

As Kelly drove them along Santa Monica Boulevard with the top down, Steve felt more excited all the time. He was aware that Mrs. Sanders had the tough job here, the waiting, the not knowing. He was going on an adventure: that would keep away the depression, the second thoughts, the worries.

The evening was balmy, perfect spring weather in other parts of the world, but pretty standard for Christmas in L.A. Cool, sweet-smelling air pummeled his face. The lights of Century City rose to one side, and on the other were the residential streets of the Beverly Hills flatlands. Kelly stopped for a red light at the corner of Wilshire and Santa Monica, where they watched the water shoot up and fall back in the colored lights of the kneeling Indian fountain.

"God, I love California," Steve said. "You know what most kids would give to drive around with the top down in December? You could sell tickets to this kind of weather."

"Yeah. We're pretty lucky, I guess." Kelly suddenly looked at Steve, and with some enthusiasm, said, "Let me drive you to New Mexico, Steve. You don't have to take the bus."

"It's not a matter of money, Kel. I want to take the bus. Besides, if you drove me, that wouldn't exactly be leaving Beverly Hills behind, would it?"

"I guess not." They drove on, and after a while, Kelly said, "The bus leaves from Hollywood at midnight, right?"

"Eleven fifty-nine."

"Right. That give us two hours to say good-bye to some people."

Brandon hated dances. There was always too much noise, too many people, too much dancing. He hated to dance.

The student parking lot was already jammed, but near some trash dumpsters he managed to find a place to leave his Mustang. It was not quite a parking area, but he didn't think he'd be in anybody's way on a Friday night.

He slammed his car door and walked across the blacktop with his hands in his pockets. He turned to walk down a wide cement aisle between tall trees. He walked toward the music. From this distance it sounded like fairy music, as if the trees themselves were playing it.

On the other side of the trees, a car pulled up and stopped. Two doors slammed and two people began to walk along the driveway that ran parallel with the promenade on which Brandon was walking.

The guy said, "This is a big deal, isn't it? Our

first big school social event together." He sounded hopeful.

"It's just a dance," the girl said. She gave the impression that she'd shrugged.

Brandon had heard that David Silver and Donna Martin were indulging in the bonding rites that culminated in two people mysteriously becoming a couple. Brandon listened to them, not really eavesdropping, but just casually, because they were all walking in the same direction.

David said, "You mean it's not weird for you to be going out with me?"

"We're not going out."

"You mean we came here together, but we're not really *together* together."

"I didn't say that." Donna sounded nervous. Could it be she really liked the guy?

"You don't have to say anything," David said with disgust. His footsteps speeded up. "Come on. Let's get it over with."

"David, wait. I'm really proud to be here with the best dancer at West Beverly High."

"Really?" David sounded delighted. There came a sudden wet smacking sound.

"David!" Donna exclaimed.

"I'm sorry," David said, as flustered as she was. "I don't know why I kissed you."

"That's okay. Let's just go to the dance, okay?"

"Okay."

At the end of the promenade, Brandon met up with David and Donna. They looked a little embarrassed, which Brandon considered to be silly. He was only the first of hundreds of people who would see them together this evening. None of them would know that David and Donna were not *together* together.

"David! Donna! So, here we are."

"Good to see you, man," David said and shook hands with Brandon. David was wearing a wild Hawaiian shirt. Donna, as usual, was very stylish in her white micro-mini. Incongruously, she wore tennis shoes with her outfit. Of course, the people at the door wouldn't let anyone into the gym in street shoes.

They went in and for a moment stood at the door peering into the dark cavernous room. Kids were gyrating to "Jingle Bell Rock," which, as was traditional at dances, played much too loud. Christmas and Hanukkah decorations alternated across the walls.

"Lots of people," David said.

"I don't see Kelly," Donna said.

"There's Chuckie," said Brandon. He was surrounded by a group of admirers who were laughing at some witticism.

"Then Kelly must be around here somewhere," Donna said, and pulled David into the gym.

As he crossed the floor to the punch table, Brandon almost knocked over Mr. Chapman, the boys' vice principal. Mr. Chapman laughed and said, "Watch it, Brandon. There's plenty of punch."

"Yes, sir. Merry Christmas, Mister Chapman."

"Merry Christmas, Brandon." They moved away from each other and into the crowd.

At the punch table, Brandon found Brenda and Dylan passing a paper cup up and back. Very romantic, if not very sanitary.

"Well, look what Santa's elves dragged in," Brenda said.

Brandon and Dylan shook hands.

Brenda beamed and exclaimed, "I love Christmas."

"Especially Christmas break," Dylan said.

"Why don't you spend Christmas with us this year?" Brandon asked. Dylan's dad was in jail. His mom was a nutroll who lived in Hawaii. He needed to spend Christmas somewhere.

Dylan shook his head and said, "I don't know."

Firmly, Brenda said, "Forget it, Dylan. You're not spending Christmas alone. And that's final."

"Okay. Just promise me your dad won't dress up like Santa Claus."

Brenda looked at Brandon and they both frowned. "Can't promise that, man," Brandon said. "Dad seems to have gone a little crazy this year. Old jingle bells got him."

Brenda said, "He's loading the garage with plastic elves, plasterboard Wise Men, stuffed camels, and fake cotton snow. Is that a mechanical sleigh I saw, Brandon?"

"A mechanical sleigh and eight tinny reindeer."

"Isn't that *tiny* reindeer?" Dylan asked.

"They look like tin to me," Brandon said.

"We can worry later about my dad's master plan for the invasion of Christmas. Come on, let's dance." Brenda grabbed Dylan by the hand and dragged him onto the dance floor. He looked back and Brandon saw a pathetic expression on his face before he disappeared into the flickering darkness.

Brandon was still sipping his first cup of punch and enjoying the sights—he could not stop himself from swaying a little to the music—when Andrea Zuckerman snuck up on him from one side. She appeared to be more serious than anyone at a dance ought to be.

"Yo, Andrea! Season's greetings," cried Brandon.

"Same to you. Listen, Brandon, you were right. That story about Chuck Wilson and Steve is one hundred percent all-beef gossip. I'm not going to run it."

That was a relief, though not a surprise. Andrea was actually kind of conservative for a crusading editor. Brandon said, "Good for you, Andrea. But just once, can we talk about something besides business?"

"Sure." Andrea rocked up and back for a moment, doing her best to move with the music. She glanced at Brandon and said, "So, do you want to dance?"

"You know I don't dance." If not dancing was

good enough for Ella Fitzgerald, Brandon
thought, it was good enough for him.

"You do, however, drink punch."

"Punch? Absolutely. I do drink punch. No
doubt about it."

Andrea picked up a paper cup and held it out.
"Well, then, Brandon, start pouring."

"Right," Brandon said, and they laughed.

"Jingle Bell Rock" continued, and pretty soon
the crowd backed off to allow David and Donna to
show their stuff. They looked great together, and
they had some very flashy moves. The song
ended, David and Donna bowed, and Donna
grabbed David. She smushed her face right into
his, gave him a big, wet sloppy kiss that was not
the kind just-friends normally bestowed on each
other.

"Hi-yo, Silver," Brandon said appreciatively.

"If that's what Donna means by platonic,"
Andrea said, "I'd be really curious to see what
she's like when she gets physical."

Donna waved at somebody in the crowd. "I
like him, see?" Donna called. "If you have a problem with that, it's just too bad."

She was waving at Kelly. Kelly grinned, and
waved back. With her other hand, Kelly was
clutching Steve Sanders's arm. Brandon was surprised to see him.

"Look," said Brandon, "there's Steve. I didn't
think he'd show, being suspended and all." He
waved at them. Steve waved back and began to

pull Kelly through the crowd toward the punch table.

"When was the last time Steve worried about a little thing like a rule?" Andrea asked.

"Hey, bro," Brandon said and gave Steve the high-five.

Chuckie marched up to them looking very angry and ignored everyone but Kelly when he said, "You stood me up. I thought we had a date."

Kelly was aloof, above whatever angry ocean Chuckie was paddling around in. She said, "I don't go out with people who hurt my friends."

Nastily, Chuckie said, "Okay for you, Ms. Taylor. If that's how you feel about it." He waded into the crowd.

Brandon did not like the ease with which Kelly had forced Chuckie to surrender. His worst fears seemed confirmed when Chuckie homed in on Mr. Chapman. Brandon saw trouble coming.

Steve nudged Kelly and said, "Watch it. Somebody might actually think you liked me or something."

Kelly pursed her lips as if doubting her own good intentions. Forcefully, almost belligerently, she grabbed Steve's hand and said, "Let's dance."

Steve and Kelly showed no daylight between them, but they had not been dancing for five seconds when Mr. Chapman approached them with Chuckie in train. Automatically, Brandon and Andrea moved in to support Steve. Brandon saw Brenda, Dylan, Donna, and David drawing closer, too. Short of indulging in physical violence, Brandon didn't know what any of them could do. More or less, a teacher's word was law. Still, Steve would feel better not being out on his limb all by himself.

Mr. Chapman said, "I hate to break this up, Steve, but you know the rules. No school, no extracurricular activities." Brandon knew Mr. Chapman. He was not a bad guy. The poor goof really sounded sorry, and maybe he was. He was trapped by the rules just the same as Steve.

"Oh, come on, Mister Chapman," Kelly said.

"I'm sorry, but you have to leave."

"Give me a break," Steve said.

"Why should he?" Chuckie asked.

Good old Chuckie. You could always count on him to say the right thing.

Steve tried hard to look only at Mr. Chapman. "I'm already suspended. What are you going to do? Expel me for coming to a dance?"

Brandon didn't believe that being sarcastic was the best approach in this instance, but the truth was, he was feeling a little sarcastic himself. Steve's crime seemed minor compared to the life-long abuse that Chuckie had heaped onto him.

"Come on, guys," Mr. Chapman said. He almost pleaded. He probably hadn't wanted to chaperon the dance in the first place. "I don't make the rules. There's no need to make a scene."

"Yes, there is," Brenda said.

Steve shook his head. "Forget it, guys. It's time for me to get on the road anyway. I have a bus to catch."

"Well, we're all going with you," Kelly said.

Echoing Brandon's own thoughts, Donna said, "We are? Where?"

"Oh, come on," Kelly said and dragged Donna away. As if Kelly and Donna were magnets and the rest of them were iron filings, Brandon and the others followed.

Chuckie called after them, "Taking buses now, Steve-o? What's the matter? Mom take away your wheels?"

Steve gently shook off Kelly and turned to face Chuckie like a gunfighter in an old western. Clint Eastwood could not have done it better. "You know what you are, Wilson?"

"No, big man. Why don't you tell me what I am?"

Chuckie was not only mean, he was evidently stupid. Brandon knew that Steve would not have asked the question unless he was ready with a good answer. After all their time together, Chuckie was not bright enough to step aside from a blow that was sure to strike him right between the eyes.

"You, Wilson, are a has-been," Steve said.

Sure enough, Chuckie was stunned. Kelly chuckled, and took Steve's arm. Steve did not stay around to enjoy Chuckie's growing discomfort but turned and walked away. All of Steve's friends followed them. David punched Chuckie in the shoulder and said, "Hang loose, dude."

Outside the gym, Dylan said, "Now that the shootout at the West Beverly Gym is over, maybe somebody will tell us what exactly is happening."

After a moment, Steve said, "Taking a bus, man. To Albuquerque. To find my real mom."

"Who's that woman you live with?" Donna asked.

"I'm adopted," Steve said.

Brandon watched astonishment bloom on the faces of his friends.

"We're going to the Hollywood bus station," Kelly said. "Steve's bus leaves at midnight—"

"Eleven fifty-nine," Steve said.

"Eleven fifty-nine," Kelly said. "And you're all invited to see him off."

"Hey, I didn't mean to drag you guys away from the dance."

Dylan said, "They were about to declare that room legally dead anyway. Besides, it's been a long time since I was in a bus station. It'll be a nice change."

"Besides," Brandon said, "I hate to dance."

"We knew that," Andrea said.

Steve shook hands all around and then spent quite a bit of time just hugging Kelly. Then he gave everyone the address of the bus station, and they formed a convoy across town with Kelly driving Steve in the lead.

As they drove east on Santa Monica

Boulevard, the city became more colorful and more depressing at the same time. Walking the streets were hustlers and victims, bag people, and the occasional tourist looking for the Hollywood of the movies but bewildered by the decay. It seemed that every other building housed a bar with a clever name and a neon martini glass hanging tilted over the door.

The bus station was on a corner next to a convenience store, an island of glare that had attracted people as shabby as it was. The walls of the building were stucco, and they had once been white. Inside, Brandon saw long lines of battered wooden chairs on a scuffed green floor. People were sleeping in them, or staring at nothing. Someone had attempted to brighten the place up with cheap Christmas ornaments but had succeeded only in emphasizing the dinginess of both the building and the ornaments. The quality of the light made everything look old and used up, even Brandon's friends. They looked pasty and wrinkled, their clothes out of place—too fancy and too colorful by half. Steve went inside to buy his ticket.

Brandon was glad to be with a big group of his friends. He felt safer with them. No doubt each of the local people had a story to tell, and many of them probably had their virtues. But knowing who could be trusted and who could not was not a job for a single evening, and making the attempt, should he desire to try, would be dangerous. Brandon believed that everyone was created equal, and that friends were where you found them, but he had to admit that these surroundings made him feel a little nervous.

Donna hugged herself against the physical and spiritual cold and said, "I can't believe I never knew he was adopted."

"Nobody knew except me and Kelly," Brandon said.

Andrea glanced into the bus station and said, "I hope he's doing the right thing."

"He's doing what he has to do," Dylan said.

Brandon nodded.

Steve and Kelly came out of the station and walked over to them.

"I have my ticket," Steve said, taking refuge in stating the obvious. He looked worried but resolute, like a man about to assault enemy territory, and perhaps, Brandon thought, that's what he was about to do.

"I hope it's a round-trip ticket," Andrea said, and smiled encouragingly.

A loud click made them jump. It was followed by an amplified cough and the voice of a man who had long ago passed disinterest and was well into boredom. He pronounced each word carefully, as if it were part of a diction lesson. "The midnight Stratocruiser to Flagstaff, Gallup, Albuquerque, Tucumcari, and Amarillo is ready for boarding at gate three."

"That's me," Steve said.

For a moment none of them moved, then they

were all hugging Steve at once. They swayed and cried and wished him good luck. Brenda sobbed, "We love you, Steve."

They fell away from him. He looked each of them in the eye and said, "I love you guys, too."

Kelly took both of his hands in hers and said, "Just remember, Steve: No matter who you find, or who you find out you are, we'll always be your family."

He hugged her one last time and picked up his overnight bag. Brandon could not ever remember feeling so sad. Tears seemed natural, and nobody remarked on them. Steve waved jauntily, then took the long walk to where the bus waited; he got in line behind a black woman carrying a string bag full of fruit and wearing a trench coat and a wool hat. Steve mounted the steps after her and walked down the aisle to a vacant seat. He waved at them again, settled his bag under his seat, and then waved again.

Brandon made a habit of trying to see the good in people, and consequently he had become Steve's best friend. He felt that Steve had already left, and he was already missing him. A support that Brandon hadn't even known was there was suddenly gone.

Brandon had no idea what Steve would find. Even if the truth was unpleasant, maybe just knowing what it was would make him happy, or at least satisfy him. Steve had the luxury of concentrating on the search ahead.

But those he left behind had only their old lives to go back to—their old lives with Steve Sanders–shaped holes in them. Not a big deal as the universe went, but big enough. It would take some getting used to.

A few minutes later the bus roared and turned into the street. A block later, it was gone.

"Let's go home," Brandon said, relieved that he had a home to go to, relieved that in an uncertain world, his parents were two people he could count on.

8

The best laid plans

BRENDA FELT THAT SHE WOULD NEVER get used to Christmas in Beverly Hills. Who ever heard of Christmas without snow? True, you didn't have to shovel sunshine, but you also couldn't sled on it, make snow angels, or have snowball fights. Beverly Hills had no snow, but it did have palm trees. Imagine!

One thing that hadn't changed was her old problem of what to buy for people she'd been buying presents for all her life. Her dad had enough ties; her mom had enough perfume; Brandon didn't need more sweat socks, not even if they had little basketballs all over them. But at least this year, she'd have her own money. She'd gotten a job at Tracy Ross, a very trendy shop on Rodeo Drive.

(Upon her arrival in Beverly Hills, one of the first things Brenda had learned was that *Rodeo* is always pronounced with the emphasis on the second syllable—Ro-DAY-oh. Never on the first. A RO-dee-oh is a place where they punch cows. Anyone who mispronounced Rodeo was at least a tourist and at worst some kind of geek.)

The sidewalks were crowded with shoppers, and each corner had its Salvation Army Santa or Mrs. Santa. Everyone was very nicely dressed. Brenda herself was confident about her appearance. She wore a dark suit with matching shoes. The shoes pinched a little and she was certain that by the end of the day she would have blisters, but what did that matter? She had a job in Beverly Hills's Golden Triangle. She was one of the beautiful people. Or, she would be waiting on them, anyway.

As she walked down Rodeo from the bus stop, she tried to ignore the palm trees and the lack of snow, and did her best to enjoy the Christmas decorations on the lampposts. Strung across the intersection of Santa Monica and Wilshire Boulevard was Santa Claus, his sleigh, and his nine reindeer—eight regular ones, and the lead with a flashing red nose. But here on Rodeo, the decking was more subtle. Each lamppost featured a group of caroling snow people under a glittering tree. Brenda guessed they looked really awesome at night.

Tracy Ross was not one of the larger stores on

Rodeo, but it had a wonderful reputation as a trendsetter, and it was very exclusive. Which meant that it was also very expensive. Which was just as well, because Brenda was working on commission. Her greed was not personal, of course. The more cunning foulard scarves she sold, the more Wild West vests, the more fake dangling earrings, the more money she'd make and the more stuff she'd be able to buy her friends and family for Christmas.

The manager of Tracy Ross, and Brenda's boss, was a woman named Diedre. She had been a model, and she still showed a lot of grace and style as she strutted around the store. The truth was, Brenda found her to be a little intimidating— she was so pretty and she knew so much about what she called "flogging the merchandise."

When she had hired Brenda, Diedre had asked her to sign a contract, the likes of which Brenda had never before seen. It was as if Tracy Ross was some kind of spy organization instead of a retail outlet. The contract asked Brenda not to talk about any of the customers, not to discuss the store's ordering practices, not to repeat anything heard anywhere on the premises. What kind of customers did they have, anyway? Dr. No? Mrs. Goldfinger?

Diedre greeted Brenda and then gave her a guided tour of the store. "The designer costume jewelry is over here." She picked up a really beautiful pair of earrings: each one looked like a pear made of pearl. "We have bios on most of the designers in the back. See?" She showed Brenda the back of the earring. Engraved there was an unreadable squiggle of a signature. "People love this stuff." She hung up the earrings and adjusted the scarfs. "Tracy's a genius about knowing what people will buy. That's why she gets to spend Christmas in Aspen with all the beautiful people while we're stuck in town flogging the merchandise."

Brenda had never been interested in retail before, but Diedre made all this seem so exciting. Maybe Brenda would have a store of her own some day.

She followed Diedre to a big round table on which small, strangely shaped bottles stood. "This is our skin care line. The Katherine Enyart Collection. She's the wife of that guy who owns the restaurant chain, you know. All her kits come prewrapped. People like that."

Diedre looked at her big blocky watch and said, "Time to rock and roll." She took a set of keys from the cash register and approached the front door.

"Thanks for the opportunity, Diedre."

Diedre shrugged. "What the hell. You needed a job. I needed a clerk. It seemed like a good idea." She opened the front door and allowed a tide of women to fill the shop.

Brenda tried to watch all the women at once. She could not decide which of them to approach first. Diedre had told her never to say, "May I help you?" but always to extend some personal compliment. "My, what a lovely sweater. We have just the scarf to match it over here." Or, "I like your hair. That style is so kicky. Here are the perfect earrings to set it off." Whatever. There was a whole lot more to sales than just making change.

She was delighted to see Kelly and Donna sweep in with the crowd, and then she felt an attack of dread. They would take all her time. Trying to be cute, they would make trouble. If Diedre saw her talking to friends, Brenda would get fired. Brenda hardened herself as they approached. She would be entirely professional. Maybe she could even sell them something. She took up a protected position behind the counter.

"What are you guys doing here?"

Kelly attempted to look innocent. "What do you mean? I love this place. It's not as expensive as Fred Hyman, but you don't have a bar either. Free soda really puts me into a buying mood." She lit up her smile. "Besides, you're the first one of my friends ever to have a real job."

Diedre glanced at them from the other side of the store, where she was showing belts to a white-haired woman in a lime-green polyester pants suit.

"Okay," said Brenda. "But you have to act like real customers." She studied Kelly and decided on a course of action. "You have such lovely features. These earrings will really set them off." Brenda felt ridiculous saying this to Kelly, but it was good practice. She pulled out a velvet tray of earrings and set them on top of the counter. "These earrings are signed," she confided.

Kelly glanced at the earrings without interest and mumbled, "Very nice." Then she leaned close to Brenda, and with great urgency, said, "You know, I'm really worried about Steve."

"He's been gone four days," Donna said.

Four days could be a lifetime. Brenda remembered the times she had been separated from Dylan. Still four days to go to Albuquerque and search for one's mother did not seem excessive.

"Nobody's heard from him," Kelly said, "His mom calls my house all the time for news. She's totally freaked."

"Maybe we shouldn't have let him go," Donna said.

"What could we do?"

"I know," Kelly said, and thought for a moment while she fingered the earrings on the counter. "It's just that—this is so weird. I really miss him. The fact that it's Christmas doesn't help."

She really looked bummed. As Kelly's friend, Brenda had to do something. "Listen you guys: Why don't you come over tonight? When Brandon gets off work, he and my dad are going to buy our tree. Maybe we can have a little tree-trimming party."

Brenda's invitation seemed to surprise the thoughts of Steve out of Kelly's head. "You haven't bought your tree yet?" Kelly said.

"We've had ours up for a week," Donna said.

"It's a family tradition. We always wait as long

as we can. That way, we always get the freshest tree."

"You guys from the Midwest really have Christmas wired, don't you?" Kelly asked admiringly.

All except the snow, Brenda thought. I really miss the snow.

Steve had been gone for a few days, and the world had slowly closed over him as it closed over anybody who left it. The Peach Pit was a zoo—what with shoppers, vacationing students, and the occasional tourist. At odd moments, Brandon wondered where Steve was, what he was doing. But Brandon had never been to Albuquerque, and had always had real parents, so he had trouble imagining what Steve's search might be like. And then the bell would ring, an order would be up, and his contemplative bubble would burst.

Nat, as usual, had gotten into the spirit of whatever was going down. He wore a felt Santa hat and forced each of his employees to wear one, too. Thinking he looked pretty dopey, Brandon didn't want to wear the hat; but after getting a few compliments from customers, he'd taken another look at himself and saw—ta-dah!—Santa Dude! Brandon raced around with orders, cracking jokes, generally sharing the Christmas spirit. He could not help feeling good.

Nat hit the bell and cried from the kitchen, "Order up, Brandon."

Brandon was coming in with new orders. He clipped them to the wheel and said, "Take it easy, Nat. Where's your Christmas spirit?"

"It goes south around cold burgers." He pulled the new orders and slapped more meat on the grill.

Brandon swooped the dishes of burgers and fries up on his arm and took them to a booth where a woman was trying to organize two giggly little girls and a pile of packages.

A guy sat down in the next booth and set his hands flat on the table. His clothes were dirty and frayed. The one old tennis shoe that stuck a little way into the aisle had no laces. The man himself seemed to be middle-aged. Rising from him was a definite odor of eau de dumpster. He had a few days' growth of salt-and-pepper beard and unkempt hair the same color. The expression on his face was neither happy nor sad but carefully neutral. On the side of his nose was a bell-shaped wart.

The guy was either a bum or a *really* eccentric millionaire, and Brandon knew which he'd bet on. The homeless were everywhere, even in the less ritzy parts of Beverly Hills, and they had a particularly bad time during this season, despite the mildness of the Los Angeles winters. Even fifty could be damned cold if you didn't have a coat. And knowing you were unloved and unwanted only made the cold bite deeper.

Still, it wasn't in Brandon to be insensitive or even impolite. Just as if the guy was really a customer, Brandon held up his pad and pencil, and asked, "What can I get for you?"

"How about a cup of joe?" the man asked in an even voice. "On the house?"

The guy was a bum, definitely. But Brandon felt sorry for him. He looked around and saw Nat setting a slice of pie in front of a customer at the counter. What would Nat say?

"I'm pretty busted," the guy said.

"Okay," said Brandon. "I'll see what I can do." He shoved his pad and pencil into an apron pocket.

"I'm pretty hungry, too."

Brandon could believe that. His face was drawn and lined like an eroded field. Brandon knew he was being hustled, but the guy really looked as if he needed help.

"I'll see what I can do," Brandon said again, and went to where Nat was wiping down the counter. He leaned close and said, "Nat, you think we could rustle up something for that guy in booth twelve? I think he might be homeless, and you know, it's Christmas."

Nat shook his head and said, "It's starting already."

"What's starting?"

"Every Christmas day I serve free dinners. Looks as if this guy came early to avoid the rush."

Like Brandon, Nat had to know he was being hustled, and he made a big show of being irritated about it. "Give him the special. But that's it—no substitutions." Brandon did not find Nat's callousness convincing. Evidently, Nat did not find it convincing either, because he immediately changed the subject. He said, "Come here. I want to show you something," and pulled Brandon into the back room.

Nat opened his locker, and from it took a Santa Claus suit. Grinning, he held it up. "I wear this every year."

Brandon was as delighted as Nat. "I bet you make a great Santa, with a sack full of burgers."

The bell rang, and Nat cried, "Order's up! Enough of this Christmas cheer!" With the Santa suit still in his hands, he rushed from the back room. He dropped the suit on the end of the counter and hurried to the window to pick up the order.

Brandon ordered the bum's special—no substitutions—and went back to work. The bum sat quietly and waited for his food, but when Brandon brought it to him a few minutes later, the bum ate quickly, as if he hadn't eaten in days. And perhaps he hadn't. Brandon did his work, and when he looked into booth twelve again, the bum was gone. In the sheen of grease left on the plate he'd written THANK YOU, making Brandon feel good all over.

When Brandon's shift was over, he went home. The Christmas trees in the lots he passed seemed sparse and dejected in the Beverly Hills heat. By the time he got home, he was not confident about finding anything worth putting up in the living room.

9

More tinsel!
More tinsel!

BUT WHEN BRANDON GOT HOME, HE SAW his dad's eagerness. The Christmas berserker frenzy was upon him. He would come back with his tree or die shopping for it. Brandon couldn't bring himself to say anything pessimistic. Instead, he said, "Hang tough, Dad. The luck of the Walshes will bring us a perfect tree."

"It's not the tree I'm worried about," Mr. Walsh said. "Look at this." He unrolled some plans on the kitchen table. Brandon and Mrs. Walsh looked at them, looked at each other speculatively, then back at the plans. Mr. Walsh pointed to the most important features as he spoke. He said, "You see? If we use a little imagination, we can have the best-decorated house on the block."

"Is that necessary, Jim?" Mrs. Walsh asked. "I mean, in Minneapolis we just threw up some lights and let Christmas spirit do the rest."

"This is Beverly Hills. Christmas spirit needs a little help."

"Right, Mom," said Brandon. "For one thing, there's no snow."

"I noticed," Mrs. Walsh said sarcastically.

"Look here," said Mr. Walsh. "The layer of artificial snow we put on the roof will not only be pretty, it will help keep our winter heating bill down."

Brandon didn't like the way he said "we."

"What heating bill?" Mrs. Walsh asked. "It's so hot out there you could grow orchids."

"Whatever. Don't you want our house to look nice?" Mr. Walsh asked, exasperated.

"You just be careful putting that sleigh on the roof. I don't want you carried off by reindeer."

"I'll wear my reindeer-proof vest," Mr. Walsh said. He rolled up his plans and said, "Come on, Brandon. Somewhere out there is a tree with our name on it."

They took Brandon's Mustang. As Brandon drove up their street, Mr. Walsh pointed out the decorations on the houses of their neighbors.

"I don't know, Dad," Brandon said. "This competitive decoration thing is pretty weird."

"We're not competing, Brandon. We're just showing a little Christmas solidarity with the neighborhood."

"Right."

"You sound like your mother."

"What can I say? It's the Walsh skepticism."

At the first place they stopped, the few trees left were dry, and their needles fell off by the handful when anyone touched them. Many of the trees were lopsided.

The tree salesman was a tall, thin man with a nose like a hatchet. He was not sympathetic. "You should have been here last week," he said. "We had some good trees last week. We spray 'em with water, but in this heat, there really isn't much we can do."

"Come on, Brandon."

"You won't do no better anyplace else," the salesman said.

Mr. Walsh just wished him a merry Christmas and kept moving.

At the second place, the same thing happened, and also at the third. By the time the Walsh men arrived at the fourth place, even Mr. Walsh was discouraged. They bought the best tree they could find—it stood up straight, anyway—but they both knew that Mom would be horrified. Brenda would probably not speak to them at all.

They got the tree home and grunting, they unloaded it. Together, they manhandled it into the living room where Mrs. Walsh frowned while she peered at it. A trail of brown needles extended between the back door and the living room.

"It looks dead," Mrs. Walsh said.

"It's just sleeping," Brandon said.

"It's not really that bad," Mr. Walsh said. "It stands up straight, anyway."

"Yes it is, Jim. It is that bad."

"If that tree stands up straight," Brandon said, "it's because of *rigor mortis*."

His father glared at him and said at last, "All right. What would you like me to do?"

"We should have gone to my mother's." Mrs. Walsh continued accusingly, "It's snowing at my mother's. And the trees are green."

Mr. Walsh took his wife into his arms and said, "Trust me, dear. It'll be a fine Christmas. You'll see."

But Mrs. Walsh would not be distracted. "Maybe. But first, we'll have to do something about that tree."

She studied the tree for a moment and then demanded that Brandon and Mr. Walsh follow her to the garage. She found a can of spray paint in a color optimistically called Forest Green, and handed it to Brandon. "Here," she said. "Make like a tree, and leaf."

Brandon and Mr. Walsh were dubious about how real a painted tree would look, but they agreed to give the spray paint a try. For one thing, the paint would hold the needles on.

Brandon started at the top of the tree. When first applied, the paint made the tree look as if it were molded from mint candy. But as it dried, the paint dulled considerably, and soon the green looked more natural. Not *really* natural, but more natural than it had. The green was an improvement over the brown, anyway.

Brandon was painting the skirt of the tree when Brenda came home from work. She screamed and demanded to know what Brandon was doing.

Feeling guilty, Brandon turned around and said, "Brenda! Home from work early, aren't you? You weren't supposed to see me doing this."

Before Brenda had a chance to reply, Mrs. Walsh came out of the house. All three of them appraised the tree. Mrs. Walsh said, "That is much better."

Brandon explained to Brenda, "Covered with tinsel, nobody's going to notice the tree. How are things on Rodeo Drive?" He said RO-dee-oh because he knew it bothered Brenda.

Brenda shook her head, but refused to rise to Brandon's bait. She only said, "Exhausting. But I made some good sales. I may even be able to buy you guys some nice stuff this year."

Mrs. Walsh said, "Remember, dear, it's the thought that counts."

Brandon nodded with all the seriousness he could muster.

"But good presents never hurt, right, Mom?" Brenda asked.

"Frankly, I find it difficult to think about Christmas when it's hot enough to be the middle of August. But I do know this: next year we'll get a fake tree." She went back into the house.

When she was gone, Brenda said, "Amazing. She must be desperate if she's considering a plastic tree."

Brandon took another few swipes at the tree with his paint, and then stood back from it to get the full effect. "So, what do you think?"

"I think we'd better use a lot of tinsel," Brenda said and went into the house.

Brandon decided she was right.

The day after the episode with the tree, a truck arrived and delivered the new house decorations Mr. Walsh had purchased. As box after box was carried from the truck, Mrs. Walsh more and more took on the appearance of someone entirely mystified by something she mistakenly had thought she completely understood. Brandon made an educated guess that the thing mystifying her at the moment was her husband.

While Mrs. Walsh's mystification grew, Mr. Walsh only became more delighted. Personally, Brandon dreaded the completion of the unloading, because he knew that when the unloading was done the setting up would begin, and that he would be shanghaied into helping his father.

Brandon and Mr. Walsh worked all morning and into the afternoon. Brandon had to admit that the sleigh on the acrylic snow on the roof looked very convincing from the front sidewalk. However, the Wise Men and assorted shepherds loitering around the stable they'd erected on the front lawn bore an uncanny resemblance to the Seven Dwarfs. Thank goodness Mr. Walsh had given up the idea of renting real camels. The plasterboard ones were just as good and lots easier to take care of.

"There," said Mr. Walsh. "Now that's a house."

The result seemed a little gaudy to Brandon, but no gaudier than some other houses on the street. Besides, if you couldn't be gaudy at Christmas, when could you?

Mrs. Walsh only commented that the house still looked unnatural without real snow.

That evening, B & B were trimming the tree with the help of Kelly, Donna, and Dylan. There was a lot of discussion about whether the tree was real or not. Brandon and Brenda kept mum, but the speculation continued. Dylan felt a needle and asked with bemused amazement whether the tree had been spray painted.

"Shut up and trim, McKay," Brandon said. "We have a lot of halls to deck and we don't want any slackers."

Dylan saluted and went back to work, but once he pointed it out, what had been done to the tree was fairly obvious. Brandon was forced to tell the whole story.

Kelly admired the ornaments until Brenda admitted that most of them had come from

Minnesota fast-food joints. But when Kelly found two big red stockings, each one embroidered with one of the twins' names, the family cover was blown. The Walshes were traditionalists to the bone. Brenda tried to convince everybody that she and Brandon hadn't put up the stockings since they were little, but nobody bought her story.

Mr. and Mrs. Walsh came into the living room with a pitcher of cold apple cider, which for a few minutes was the center of attention. Mr. Walsh admired the progress the kids had made on the tree, though Mrs. Walsh seemed to remain unconvinced that it was the Christmas tree of her dreams. Brandon didn't think she'd ever really be able to enjoy that tree, no matter how much of it they hid with decorations.

While everybody else sipped cider, Mrs. Walsh said brightly, "Listen, you guys: Back in Minneapolis, we'd always hold these huge Christmas Eve dinners. We'd invite the whole family and all our friends. We'd exchange gifts and sing Christmas carols. And the party would always end with a huge snowball fight in the back-yard." She smiled and made big pictures in the air with her hands.

"Snowball fight?" Donna asked with disbelief.

Mrs. Walsh saw the problem, and said, "Maybe we won't have a snowball fight this year. But in honor of our first Christmas in Beverly Hills, I'd like to invite all of you and your families to spend

Christmas Eve here. So we can begin a new tradition." She nodded at her husband. He nodded back. They watched the crowd expectantly.

Brandon could see that this idea did not come from the top of his mom's head. It was something that his parents had cooked up together. Perhaps it had even been Dad's idea, to make Mom feel better about the tree and the lack of snow. For some reason, however, the idea did not go over very well.

As if admitting she had a terrible disease, Donna said that she and her family were going to ski up at Mammoth Mountain over Christmas.

Kelly seemed not much happier to explain that for the first time in recorded history her mother was going to cook Christmas dinner. "David Silver and his father are coming over. I don't get it, but Mom really likes David Silver's father."

Without apologies, Dylan said that he was going to spend Christmas with his father, in the visitor's pen of the local minimum-security prison. "Sorry, Bren."

"That's okay," Brenda said. She tried to hide her disappointment, but Brandon could see how hurt she was.

"Wait a minute," Mr. Walsh said. "Aren't we missing somebody? Where's Steve?"

The squirming Brandon had observed when Mrs. Walsh extended her invitation was nothing to the squirming caused by Mr. Walsh's question. Nobody felt comfortable with the subject, yet the question needed to be answered. Steve's secret was now public knowledge, at least among his immediate circle of friends. There was no reason Brandon's mom and dad shouldn't know. So he told them. They seemed somewhat less astonished than he'd expected. Was it possible they'd known all along?

Kelly said, "I wonder what he's doing right now?"

Steve felt that he'd been sitting on this bus seat all his life, and was taking on its contours. He was stiff and cold and in need of food. The bus had a bathroom, and he had used it a time or two—on a sixteen-hour trip it was unavoidable—but being a gymnast and a contortionist would have helped. By contrast, the bathrooms on most commercial jets were roomy.

As he'd ridden through the night, he slept fitfully, trying to ignore the noise of the engine and of other people trying to sleep around him, trying to ignore the smell of ancient cigarette smoke and of combusting diesel fuel. Sleeping sitting up was never a success, and because Steve could find nowhere to wedge his feet, he kept sliding down. He awoke to find, with some surprise and embarrassment, that he'd been resting his head on the shoulder of the stranger next to him.

She was a cute girl going home to Albuquerque for Christmas, and under other circumstances,

Steve might have made a play for her. But he was on a serious mission and uncertain about his future. He was in no mood for a fling.

She was understanding about his leaning on her, and they had a real conversation. Without shame, Steve inflicted his story on her. He just talked to hear his own voice, for the company. Thank goodness the girl had been sympathetic.

The sun came up and illuminated mountains and then deserts, all of which had the most astonishing colors and rugged forms. He might have been riding across the face of another planet instead of just another time zone. The scenery was beautiful but monotonous.

And still the bus went on. Looking at a map, even flying, one got little sense of how large the United States actually was. To get the full impact, one needed to cross the country on the ground, like a bug crossing a table. No doubt walking would be even more of an education, but Steve would gratefully forego that experience.

The bus arrived in Albuquerque at about five in the afternoon, mountain standard time. It being winter, the sun was already on the horizon, and he was in a neighborhood where he did not care to spend the night.

But he had plenty of money, not to mention credit cards. He hired a cab, and on the driver's recommendation, went to the Valdes Motor Inn. He was surprised at how little time it took to cross town.

The Valdes Motor Inn was clean but not

fancy. It would do. Steve was only going to sleep
there and use the phone book to plot his next
move. Albuquerque had only one major hospital,
and Steve would visit it the next day. He had a
greasy burger in the coffee shop next door to the
inn, not a patch on Nat's, and went back to his
room.

As Steve fell asleep, he imagined that his body
was still vibrating to the rhythm of the bus. The
feeling was eerie and not entirely unpleasant. The
sounds coming from the nearby highway added
to the illusion that the bed was moving. He was so
keyed up he didn't think he'd ever fall asleep, but
he slept soundly and was awakened in the morning by the horn of a truck attempting to encour-
age the slow car ahead of it.

After breakfast, he took another cab to the
hospital, and after waiting his turn, he finally got
to speak with the nun behind the counter. She
was friendly, and Steve was certain that he was
home free. She'd asked for identification, and he'd
given her his driver's license. She'd taken it with
her into a back room.

In a matter of moments, he would know
where his real mother was. After that, a short cab
ride would take him to her. His entire life would
change. He played with the pencil on the counter
until another nun, this one typing into a computer,
looked at him questioningly.

The first nun came back with a folder. That
must be it, Steve thought excitedly. Inside was his

past and maybe his future. She did not put the folder onto the counter, but clutched it to her bosom.

"Is that it?" Steve asked, afraid of any answer he might receive.

"It appears to be," the nun said. She was neither pleased nor disappointed. The folder simply *was*. She handed him his driver's license with an air of finality that Steve did not like.

"Let me see," Steve said.

The nun would not look at him. She fingered the file and said, "I didn't realize you were not yet eighteen. Under the circumstances, I'll need written permission from your mother before I can show you the record."

This can't be happening, Steve thought. He felt sick. He said, "Look, uh, Sister. I traveled a long way to get here. I came by bus, so you know it wasn't a pleasure trip. Can't you make an exception just this once? It'll be our secret."

"I'm sorry."

She really sounded sorry, but that wasn't good enough. He pointed out, "If I knew where my mother was, I wouldn't need the folder."

The nun just shook her head. Steve tried to make a donation to her favorite charity, but that only shocked her so much that she retreated a step from the counter.

He turned away from the counter, dejected, disgusted, utterly whipped. He sat down and tried to come up with an alternate plan, but there was too much blackness in his brain. He rested his head in his hands.

"Here."

Steve looked up and saw the nun holding the folder out to him. For a second he didn't understand what was happening.

"You can look at it," the nun said primly, "but I can't let it leave the room."

Steve took the folder eagerly, thanked the nun, and with shaking hands, opened the folder. He closed his eyes, then opened them and read:

STEVEN BROWN
Born this fifteenth day of May in Albuquerque, New Mexico, to Karen Brown.

It was him! It was really him! He'd been born! Wait a minute. Get a grip. Of course he'd been born. Everybody was born. What else? Steve found out that he'd been a big baby—nine pounds, eleven ounces—which for some reason pleased him. And there in black and white was Karen Brown's address. On a slip of paper he hastily wrote 5595 Navajo Trail. He gave the folder back to the nun, blessed her—which immediately struck him as presumptuous—and left as quickly as he could.

Outside, the air was bright and cold, an amazingly stimulating combination. All was right with the world. Steve hired a cab, gave the address as if he were going to Buckingham Palace, and they

were off. Steve fought an impulse to explain everything to the driver. But no, he would just savor the
knowledge that he was going to meet his real
mother at last. Would she like him? Would he like
her? Film at eleven. Film in about fifteen minutes.

They drove along busy streets, and Steve
expected at any moment to turn into a quiet, tree-
lined neighborhood, with clean but modest houses and kids playing baseball in the street. He was
surprised when the cab pulled into the parking lot
of a shopping center.

"What's this?" Steve asked.

"This is your address, 5595 Navajo Trail," the
driver said.

"But I'm looking for a house."

"There used to be some houses here. But that
was a long time ago."

Steve didn't understand why this was happening to him. He'd come so far, had overcome so
many obstacles, to arrive at this dead end. If he
were the type who gave up, he would have wondered if somebody—the nun's Boss?—didn't want
him to meet his real mother. But Steve had never
wanted anything so much in his life: not clothes,
not cars, not women. He knew he had to go on,
but he'd never had so little notion how to continue. He started by asking the driver to take him
back to the Valdes Motor Inn.

10

A stack of quarters

TRACY ROSS WAS BUSY. BUT BRENDA would rather be busy than bored, and her commissions were adding up. She thought it interesting that shoppers showed their Christmas spirit in different ways. Some were so frantic they'd buy anything in their price range. Others found a problem with everything Brenda showed them. Still others were friendly and ready to be helped.

Once, a guy in a Santa suit came in handing out candy canes. On the side of his nose was a bell-shaped wart. He seemed jolly enough, but Diedre reacted as if he were carrying the plague. She wasn't very polite, either. Brenda had to admit the guy looked thin, and apparently had not shaved lately, but she felt bad when Diedre threw him out. The guy was only temporarily discouraged, and he wished Diedre a merry Christmas as he was pushed out the door.

Later, Dylan came in and pretended to be interested in some hats while Brenda finished waiting on a customer. She knew that the customer was not getting her full attention. Part of her was really pleased when people visited her at work. It meant she hadn't been forgotten. But the arrival of friends made doing a good job more difficult. Brenda couldn't talk to her friends without fearing she would be caught by Diedre.

It always thrilled her to see Dylan. She came over and picked up a hat as if she were showing him its finer points. It had a wide brim that was turned up in the front to sport a big silk flower.

He handed her a candy cane. "Don't eat it," Dylan said. "It's probably poisonous. Some shabby Santa Bum pushed it into my hand."

"Did he have a bell-shaped wart on his nose?"

"I didn't notice. Or is that code?"

Brenda could explain, but it didn't seem important. She said, "I thought you left."

"Without saying good-bye? Are you kidding?" He took a small white box from his jacket pocket and handed it to her.

Brenda was desperate to know what was inside, but she was in a public place, and besides, Dylan might ask her not to open it till Christmas.

He said, "Open it if you want."

She grinned and pulled off the top. Inside, resting on a square of cotton, was half a golden heart on a chain. "Dylan, it's beautiful. But where's the other half?" She knew where it was, but she wanted to hear Dylan tell her.

He said, "Right here." He opened his palm to reveal the other half of the heart.

They hugged and proclaimed undying love for each other. Brenda had no doubt that this time it would stick. After all, true love always stuck eventually. Overwhelmed by the moment, she offered to go with him when he visited his father in jail.

"No. You need to spend Christmas with your family. Besides, it'll be the first time I've seen him since they put him away. We have a lot to talk about."

"Yeah." Brenda nodded. He was right. She wouldn't be selfish. There would be lots of other holidays. Part of being in love was giving the other person their space. She'd seen that in the newspaper. The fact that letting go a little was difficult didn't mean doing it wasn't worthwhile.

Their good-bye was not as leisurely as Brenda would have wished. Customers crowded around demanding her attention. One of them wanted Brenda to put away a particularly ugly blouse so she could buy it for cheap during the after-Christmas sale that was sure to come. Brenda didn't think this would fly with Diedre, and it didn't.

■   ■   ■

The Peach Pit was between the lunch rush and the dinner rush. Business was only busy instead of insane, and Brandon had time to do his side work. He filled shakers and dispensers and swept the floor.

Andrea came in while Brandon was wiping down a table recently vacated by a couple who'd had ice cream sodas and left him a nickel tip. Cheapskates. She looked glum, which was amazing considering Christmas and the fact that school would be out for another week. But Brandon was dealing with Andrea here. She frequently did not see things the way other people did.

"Peach pie, Andrea?" Brandon asked. She ate pie only when she was depressed. Dessert played hob with her diet. She was always on a diet.

Andrea nodded.

"À la mode?"

Andrea nodded.

"This is serious," Brandon said as he dished up her pie and ice cream. "Tell all."

"It's Christmas, Brandon."

Brandon nodded and put down the plate in front of her. She stared right through it. "I understand. The Jewish thing."

"That's only part of it." She took up her spoon and began to pry away chunks from around the edges, first of the pie and then of the ice cream. "My family never celebrated Hanukkah either. My parents figured it would be easier if we didn't celebrate anything."

Brandon was about to make a comment about this being a clever way for parents to avoid giving presents, but Andrea was bummed enough without his humorous asides. He was pleased to find that he had a better idea. He said, "Mom's dying to play hostess. Why don't you come for dinner Christmas Eve?"

This had the opposite effect from the one Brandon had anticipated. Andrea became more depressed. She said, "I can't. I already promised my grandmother I'd go to the movies with her. She loves to go to the movies on Christmas Eve because there aren't any lines."

"Bring her."

"Christmas is not exactly her thing. If you know what I mean."

While Brandon was thinking about Andrea's dilemma, Nat came out of the back room and asked, "Brandon, have you seen my Santa suit?"

"Not since that day you showed it to me."

"It's gone."

Andrea asked the question that had been in Brandon's mind. "Who'd be tacky enough to steal a Santa suit?"

"Yeah," Nat said.

Steve sat in his motel room for a long time watching the traffic go by. After a while, the answer came to him, but he didn't like it. Just to see if the answer was really as hideous as he imagined, he opened the phone book. There were three pages of Browns. He sighed. He didn't mind working to solve his problem—he'd come all the way to Albuquerque on a bus, after all—but what he had to do now would be a killer. It would be a different kind of ordeal from a sixteen-hour bus ride, but it would be just as harrowing.

He sighed and went down the block, where he bought a roll of quarters at a bank. Forty quarters. Forty chances to find out what he needed to know.

He went to one of the three public phones in the lobby of the Valdes Motor Inn and cracked open his roll of quarters as if it were an egg. He stacked them and then opened the phone book. Three pages of Browns. Sheesh! He put a quarter into the telephone and called the first number.

"Hello?" It was the voice of a woman. Good. He was always good with women.

Steve said, "Hello. I'm looking for a Karen Brown, or a relative of Karen Brown. She gave birth to a son seventeen years ago."

The woman didn't say anything. She just hung up.

"Jerk," Steve said. He put another quarter into the telephone and called the second number.

"Hello?"

"Hello. I'm looking for . . ." He went on.

The second person was a man. He had no idea what Steve was talking about but wished him a merry Christmas.

Steve dialed the third number.

He lost track of how many Browns he called, but he saw that he was running out of quarters. Worse yet, his frustration and depression crept into his voice. More and more, people reacted badly to him, as if he were trying to sell them something unclean.

"Hello?" It was the voice of a crusty old man. These guys not only hung up on him, they generally said something insulting before they did it. Steve wondered if he should even bother asking the question.

He said, "Hello. I'm looking for a Karen Brown, or a relative of Karen Brown. She gave birth to a son seventeen years ago."

Suddenly angry, the man said, "Who is this? What do you want?"

Steve became excited. With new enthusiasm, he said, "I'm somebody who needs to talk with her. This is very important." He could not tell this stranger the whole story. Not yet. "I'm her son," seemed a bit abrupt.

Steve heard breathing at the other end, and the clatter of dishes. He looked at the phone book. He was talking to somebody at Brown's Cafe, 89403 Red Rock Way. Why didn't the idiot speak up?

There was a loud click, and the phone went dead. Numb, Steve listened to the silence. The guy had hung up. Steve hung the receiver on the hook. This was it, Steve was certain. Otherwise, why would the guy act so strange? This had to be it. Steve gathered up the few remaining quarters, then ran outside to hail a cab.

11

Simple gifts

AS CHRISTMAS APPROACHED, BUSINESS AT Tracy Ross became more frantic. Then Brenda noticed that no one had come into the shop for quite a while. She could actually hear the recorded Christmas music whispering from hidden speakers. Oh, the occasional shop-shocked customer still staggered in, bought the first thing that caught his or her eye, with some relief crossed a name off a list, and hurried out. But most people had already done their shopping. The streets and sidewalks were nearly empty, and growing emptier by the moment. Brenda sighed. She loved Christmas, and here it was nearly upon them at last.

Diedre was in the back, adding up receipts,

fixing her makeup, or something. She really was an awesome sales person, even if she did have a tendency to take over Brenda's sales as she was about to close them. Maybe it was just instinct on Diedre's part, but Brenda wished she would stop. Brenda had lost a couple of nice commissions that way. Diedre always took the commission.

Brenda, who was in need of company, was pleased to see Kelly come in, but Kelly looked awful. Her eyes were red, as if she'd been crying, and she hadn't dressed with her usual care. She stood at the door, seemingly confused, and then saw Brenda.

Brenda went to her and with some concern, asked what was wrong.

Kelly smiled a weak and nervous smile, and seemed on the verge of falling into her arms. She said, "I had to talk to somebody, Bren. Donna's in Mammoth, you know."

"I love being second choice."

"Oh, Bren, that's not what I meant." She did fall into Brenda's arms then, and started to cry. "I don't know what I mean. Christmas is awful."

Brenda could see that Kelly was in no mood for kidding, and for a while, just patted her on the back and told her that everything was going to be all right. "Is it Steve?" Brenda asked.

"What?" Kelly seemed surprised at the question. "No. We haven't heard from him. No, it's David Silver's father, the formerly perfect Mel." She sniffed and pulled a shred of tissue from her pocket.

"Formerly perfect?"

"He came over last night and told my mom that he wants to get back together with his wife for Christmas. My mom cried for hours."

"Oh my goodness." Brenda could comfort Kelly, but short of convincing Mel Silver to snap out of it, there was nothing else to be done.

"Goodness had nothing to do with it." Kelly shook her head and dabbed at her eyes. "I don't know why, Bren, but Mom really liked that guy." Kelly shuddered as she sighed. "Now, she never wants to see him again. Hell of a Christmas present, huh?"

"Not my first choice."

"No. But what I'm really worried about is that Mom is so depressed that she might start drinking again."

An idea came to Brenda with such force, it was almost a physical blow. She could do something useful after all. She smiled and said excitedly, "Why don't you come to our house Christmas Eve?"

"Really? I mean, it's such short notice."

Kelly was right about that, and Brenda felt a sudden pang of worry. But she convinced herself—with justification, she thought—that her mom would be delighted. "Mom always cooks for an army. And she loves company. Especially during the holidays."

Kelly smiled as if she meant it and said, "We'll bring dessert. My mom actually made this incredible chocolate mousse. You won't believe it." She giggled. "Mel Silver almost ended up wearing it."

A man in a Santa suit came in and gave each of them a candy cane. He looked like the guy Dylan had called Santa Bum, the same one Diedre had chased out of the shop earlier. He even had the same bell-shaped wart on the side of his nose. Brenda wondered where a guy like this got candy canes. Did he steal them? Brenda found that difficult to believe. He seemed like such a nice old geezer, and so full of the spirit of Christmas.

Diedre shot out of the back room like a pinball out of the chute and angrily chased him away again. Brenda felt bad for the guy, but without endangering her job she didn't feel that she could contradict Diedre.

"Creep," Diedre grumbled as the door closed behind Santa Bum. After he was gone, Diedre spotted Kelly and turned the charm back on. "Looking for that perfect last-minute gift?"

"Uh, no," Kelly said. "See you later, Brenda."

While she fluffed the scarfs, Diedre said, "I hope you're not taking work time to yak with your friends."

Brenda wondered what the problem was. She hadn't seen a customer for forty-five minutes. But she smiled and said, "No. Kelly just came in to wish me a merry Christmas."

"That's nice," Diedre said and ducked into the back room.

It was too bad that Kelly's mom and Mel Silver were breaking up, but at least Kelly and

Brenda would be able to spend Christmas together. Now all they needed was Donna and Dylan.

Being given a nickel tip was unusual at any time, but at Christmas it almost never happened. Brandon was a good waiter, and at Christmas that meant he collected bigger tips from people who were full of the spirit of giving.

Brandon took advantage of a lull in the action to give Nat a little something. It was a peach-shaped apron with the words "The Pit Rules" embroidered on it. As Brandon had hoped, Nat loved the gift. And Nat returned the favor by handing Brandon an envelope full of cash, which he called "a little thank you for being such a good employee all year."

Brandon had not expected a Christmas bonus, but he was pleased to accept it. Car insurance was not exactly cheap. He asked Nat, "You want to come for Christmas dinner? We'd love to have you."

"Thanks for the invite, but my cousin is expecting me." He looked at his watch and affected a gruff tone. "You better get out of here. At the moment, I'm sure your mom needs you more than I do."

"You sure?"

"I'm the boss, right? Of course I'm sure."

"Thanks, Nat."

While whistling "White Christmas" Brandon changed his pants and shirt, and took another present from his locker. He smiled when he thought of who it was for. Leaving early would allow Brandon to deliver it now rather than having to shoehorn it in among the Walsh Christmas festivities.

As he drove across town to the hospital, he wondered for the hundredth time if he was doing the right thing. Dealing with sick people was never easy for him, and when the sickness was psychological rather than physical, in some ways dealing with the person was even more difficult. How to act and what to say were high on his list of questions.

Despite Brandon's discomfort, he felt that making the pilgrimage across town was not only important but necessary. Emily was still important to him, and he didn't want her to feel that she was all alone on Christmas.

Emily Valentine was a cute blonde who had almost immediately become popular among the guys when she arrived at West Beverly. She had a reputation for being a wild woman, and she could, with equal ease, talk about car engines or make-up. The problem was that she became obsessed with Brandon, and at last, tried to get his complete attention by setting fire to a homecoming float.

Which explained her presence in the psychiatric ward.

Brandon found her in the ward's lounge reading a magazine. He was relieved to see that she was the same Emily, same semipunk hairstyle, same pert little face, same pixie smile. But she seemed somehow calmer than when Brandon had seen her last. Despite her excitement and happiness at seeing Brandon, she maintained a psychological distance from him and protected a quiet center.

Grinning, Brandon handed her the present.

She tore off the Christmas paper and held up what was inside. "It's your Minnesota Twins shirt!" Emily cried.

Brandon tried to be casual. "Yeah, well, it's my favorite shirt, but you always liked it, so I figured—"

"You're not getting this back, you know."

"I know," Brandon said gently. "Look at the card."

Emily found the card taped to the paper. She opened it and read out loud, "Merry Christmas from all your good friends at West Beverly: Dylan, Kelly, Steve, Andrea, Donna, David, Brenda, and Brandon."

Brandon was tearing up, and he saw that Emily was crying, too. Brandon felt awkward, and he attempted to lighten things up. He said, "So, you should hear what's going on between David Silver and Donna Martin."

They talked for half an hour, and when Brandon had to leave, he felt good about having come. He had looked upon the face of his own fear and lived, he had done a nice thing for Emily, and he found out that they still liked each other. Emily wouldn't be in that place forever, and when she was released, a date was definitely not out of the question.

■ ■ ■

Steve took a cab to the edge of town. The ride seemed to take forever. Then, on a corner lot surrounded by an ancient square of asphalt that was presently empty, he found a small whitewashed building with a weathered sign over the door: *Brown's Cafe*. At least it was still here, Steve thought with relief. He was a long way from Beverly Hills.

He paid off the cab and walked through the cold bright late afternoon air to the building. He was excited and afraid. He could not begin to guess what he might find out inside.

A bell tinkled when he opened the door. Ceiling fans slowly stirred the warm greasy atmosphere. The decor came from the same era as the Peach Pit: booths lined one wall; along the other was a long counter with round stools whose tops matched the red plastic in the booths; behind the counter was a polished stainless steel wall and the window into the kitchen. Steve could see a tall black man through the window; he wore a white paper hat and tapped his spatula lightly against the griddle.

A man was sitting at the counter sipping coffee. He looked over his shoulder when Steve came in. The face was curious but not entirely unfriendly. It was round as the moon and had seen as much hard use. As the man stood up, he said, "Howdy. What can I get for you?"

It occurred to Steve that he hadn't eaten for many hours. Well, that could wait. He tried to see a resemblance between himself and this large solid man. Maybe the man wasn't even a Brown. Maybe he was just hired help. Steve asked, "Is this your place?"

Immediately, the man became suspicious. Only tax collectors, process servers, and other sources of trouble asked such a question. He admitted that it was.

"Please," Steve pleaded, "I need your help. I need to find Karen Brown."

"You're the nut who called a while ago."

"Yes. Do you know her or not?" Steve sounded frantic and impatient. Maybe he was a little nutty by now.

The man made a decision. Angrily, he said, "Of course I know her. I'm her father. What's it to you?"

Karen Brown's father. The old guy was his grandfather. Oh, my gosh. Steve felt his composure drifting away. Any minute he'd be hugging this stranger and balling like a little kid. Get a grip, Steve. Quietly, he said, "I'm her son."

The man froze and stared at Steve wide-eyed. Then, affecting a casual attitude, he asked, "Want some coffee?"

"Absolutely," Steve said. "Absolutely."

The man brought two cups of coffee to an empty booth near the door. They sat down and the rest of the room faded from Steve's notice. He was aware only of the man's face and of his voice. The coffee cooled before him, untouched.

"Call me Al," the man said. He had a clean, hard voice, a pioneer voice. It was old but still strong.

"Al," Steve said, liking the sound of it. He also liked Al's directness. "Call me Steve."

Al smiled and said, "I know your name. I helped name you."

"You did?" Steve was delighted.

"I did." Al sipped coffee.

"So, does Karen, my mother, still live around here."

"Not anymore," Al said sadly. He shook his head and looked deep into his cup.

Steve had so many questions he didn't know which one to ask first. He said, "Why didn't she keep me, Al?"

Al looked into the distance, seeing the past as he spoke. "Your mom was very young when you were born, still in high school. And she didn't have a husband. Not then. She wanted her baby to have a good home, with a family that had the resources to take care of him. Was it a good home, Steve?"

For the first time since boarding the bus, Steve thought about his mother, Mrs. Sanders, the woman he'd left alone for Christmas back in Beverly Hills. He missed her terribly, with a longing as strong as his curiosity about Karen Brown. If there was any way for a person to be in two places at once, Steve would have managed it.

"Steve?" Al asked.

"Yeah, Al. It was a good home. What did she do after high school?"

"She went to college in Albuquerque, met a nice young man and got married."

"Wow. So that's why I couldn't find her in the book. She changed her name."

"Right. To Mulligan."

If she'd kept him, Mulligan would have been Steve's stepfather. Wow. "Did she talk about me, Al? Did she ever think about me?"

Al shrugged and made a considering face. "In her private moments I'm sure she did. But not around her family."

Steve noticed the coffee and took a sip. It was strong and still hot. He needed to ask the big question. He was afraid to ask it and afraid not to ask it. Still, he would be silly to have come all this way and not go a little farther. He said, "Would you give me her number, Al? I don't know why, but I have this strong feeling I should be with her at Christmas. I want to meet her. I want to know my real mother, and I want her to know me."

Al met Steve's eyes and said simply, "Karen's dead, Steve."

"What?" Steve's shock was mingled with a relief he didn't want to admit. She would never love him, but she would never hate him either.

"Ten years ago she was in a real bad car accident. It happened just a few blocks from here."

Steve couldn't speak. The coffee splashed and burned him. He put down the cup with shaking hands.

"I'm sorry," Al said. "I know she would have

wanted to see you. Wait here a minute."

Steve waited. He didn't want to move. It took all his energy just to get used to the idea that Karen Brown was dead. Al came back with some old snapshots in an envelope. One was Karen Brown's high school graduation picture. Another showed her in a wedding dress standing next to a guy who must be Mulligan. Handsome dude. Karen was beautiful, and she had curly blond hair just like his. Steve could not help smiling.

The smile went away and Steve asked to see Karen's grave. Al nodded, told the cook he'd be back soon, and took Steve to a cemetery in an old International pickup truck that may once have been red. On the way, Steve bought a small bouquet of flowers, nothing fancy. Steve felt that Karen Brown would have been embarrassed at anyone fussing over her too much.

Al parked outside the cemetery fence, and they walked inside through the tall gates. It was colder than it had been, and the sun was going down through high pink clouds. Al knew right where the grave was. He must have come here often. Steve knelt by the grave and carefully set down the flowers. The funny thing was that the longer he stood there, the more certain Steve became that Karen Brown was no longer under that sod. Oh, her bones and stuff were undoubtedly there. But her goodness and warmth were inside Steve—in his memory, and in Al's.

Without looking up, Steve said, "I always

thought that if I met my real mom, things would be different. I would, like, know where I fit in."

"You seem to fit in pretty good right where you are," Al said.

Steve considered that, and decided Al was right. There was nothing more for him here. He needed to get home. Home with his mother. Can't let Mom spend Christmas alone. He stood up.

Steve smiled and said, "Maybe in fifty years, I'll look like you."

"If you're lucky." Al chuckled.

A moment later it occurred to Steve that there might be something here for him, after all. He said, "I never had a grandfather before. Would *you* be my grandfather, Al?"

After a moment of deliberation, Al said, "I'd be honored."

He turned and walked slowly toward the gates. Steve caught up and they walked together. With suddenly energy, he said, "We'll keep in touch. I'll send you Christmas cards and maybe one day you'll come to L.A. for a visit."

"Sure," Al said. "We'll see what happens."

He doesn't believe me, Steve thought, but I can't let my first and only grandfather get away. I *will* keep in touch. "Sure," said Steve. "We'll see what happens."

They wished each other a merry Christmas.

They got back into the truck and the doors swung shut with a pair of clangs. As the engine started, Steve was struck by the fact that the next day was Christmas, and that he didn't have time to take the bus back to L.A. He also didn't have anything to think over. He knew who his mom was.

He asked Al to drive him to the airport. "I have to get home.

Al nodded and eased the truck into gear.

It was Christmas, and all the commercial carriers would probably be booked. Unless he was very lucky or could charter a plane, Steve would be stuck in Albuquerque for a day or two, at least. Before, it had seemed very important that he know his real mother. Now, it seemed even more important that he not disappoint the woman who'd raised him.

12

A visit from St. Nicholas

BRANDON WAS SITTING IN THE LIVING ROOM awash in warm Christmas feelings. Dad played "God Rest Ye Merry Gentlemen" on his chord organ while the smells of roasting turkey and baking cookies wafted from the kitchen. There were few smells that so fed the soul as well as whetted the appetite. Meanwhile, Brandon read "A Christmas Carol" by Charles Dickens. The old boy certainly had a traditional Christmas down pat. No wonder the best Christmases were described as Dickensian.

It was a pleasure to just lie around. The Peach Pit was closed for the holiday; and after weeks of calling all over the city, Brandon and his father had finally finished preparing the big Christmas surprise for Cindy Walsh. If Mrs. Walsh loved the result, then all the hard work had been worthwhile. But Brandon was afraid that the surprise would just make her more homesick than she already was. Mr. Walsh told Brandon not to worry and went on playing the organ. He was now into "We Three Kings of Orient Are."

Brandon worried anyway. Of course, the surprise was only one of the things he had on his mind. The other was Steve. Nobody had heard from him since he left, and it was much too easy to imagine bizarre and terrible reasons for his silence.

The front doorbell rang, which surprised Brandon because everybody they knew claimed to be busy for Christmas. His mom answered the door, and let in Samantha Sanders, Steve's mom. Mrs. Sanders seemed upset. Her eyes were red from crying and she could not keep still. When Mr. Walsh saw her, he stopped playing and listened intently.

At first, Mrs. Walsh seemed a little nervous talking to a big celebrity, but her nervousness soon dissolved into genuine concern. Mrs. Sanders had not heard from Steve for a week. Had Steve contacted them?

"I haven't heard anything," Mrs. Walsh said. "Brandon?"

"Not a peep," Brandon said. He thought it best not to share his pulp-fiction fantasies. Brandon knew Mrs. Sanders had been through a lot lately, what with turning down the reunion show and then losing Steve, if only temporarily.

"I called the police," Mrs. Sanders said. "They're going to file a missing person's report in a few hours." She shook her head as if to clear it. "I suppose Steve told you where he was going. And why."

"He did," Brandon said.

His mom looked on anxiously while Mrs. Sanders paced in the foyer. "I can't believe he wouldn't even call," Mrs. Sanders said. "That's why I'm so scared."

Brandon wondered if his nightmares and Mrs. Sanders's nightmares matched.

Mrs. Sanders continued to pace. "When Steve was little, he'd have so many Christmas presents that by the time he'd opened them all, he'd be too exhausted to play with anything." She stopped, stared at Mrs. Walsh and said, "Maybe that's it," she said piteously. "Maybe I gave him too many presents. I don't know. I know I did *something* wrong."

"No parent is perfect," Mrs. Walsh said. "But Steve is a wonderful boy. You must have done a lot right, too."

But Mrs. Sanders was too engrossed in beating herself over the head to accept compliments. She put her hand on the knob of the front door and said, "Maybe. Look, I'm sorry to bother you with this on Christmas. If he calls here, please let me know. I'll be at home."

Mrs. Walsh grabbed her by the arm and said, "You won't get away that easily. I have an enormous turkey in the oven and somebody has to help us eat it. You're staying for Christmas dinner."

Mrs. Sanders politely declined the invitation, but Brandon didn't buy it. The woman could have used the phone to ask about Steve. The fact that she'd come all the way over here meant that she actually wanted to be here. Brandon knew what the outcome of the little drama would be before it played itself out. Mrs. Walsh insisted she stay, and Mrs. Sanders at last capitulated. "But just for dinner," she said. "I have to be home in case Steve calls."

That seemed to satisfy Mrs. Walsh. The two women went into the kitchen together.

"Another new Christmas tradition," Mr. Walsh said. "TV stars for dinner." He began to bumble through an awkward rendition of "Santa Claus Is Coming to Town." Brandon went back to Dickens and tried not to listen.

Brenda had one of the most difficult mornings of her life. Because Tracy Ross had been so quiet the day before, she had assumed that everyone had already finished their Christmas shopping.

But Tracy Ross was open on Christmas Eve morning, and many frantic people had taken advantage of it. Business was so brisk that Diedre was happy getting commissions on just her own sales. At noon they had to throw people out of the store before they could close. Brenda straightened merchandise and dusted as Diedre rang out the cash register. When Diedre opened the door to let them leave, she said, "If you think today was crazy, wait till you see what it's like on the twenty-sixth when everything goes on sale."

"Terrific."

Diedre locked the door and set the alarm. Then she astonished Brenda by kissing her on both cheeks like a movie Frenchman. After that, Diedre walked away without a look back.

Brenda walked quickly toward the bus stop, eager to get home. Dad would be playing carols on the organ and plates of candy and cookies would be all over the place. Because of the heat, she couldn't bundle into a warm woolly sweater, of course, but it would be great being home. Christmas at the Walshs' was always great. A two-thousand-mile move couldn't change that.

At the corner of Rodeo and Brighton Way, Brenda saw a couple of policemen urging a scrawny Santa Claus into a police car. Both policemen were young and kind of cute; one of them had a tiny mustache, just a baby. Santa wished them merry Christmas and held out candy canes he took from a big sack that may once have belonged to the post office. It was bulky, and obviously had more than candy canes in it. Neither policeman was amused by his offer.

For a moment, Brenda was astonished by this vision. Then she saw that the Santa was the man Dylan had called Santa Bum, the one with the bell-shaped wart on his nose, and she became angry. What right did these policemen have to hassle any Santa, let alone her own personal Santa Bum?

She walked over to them and said, "I know this guy."

The policemen looked at her with surprise, but Santa only gazed at her mildly, as if he'd been expecting her to save him.

The policeman with the baby mustache said, "We got a complaint from somebody at Tracy Ross, says this guy is bothering shoppers."

More of Diedre's work. Brenda didn't know if she could bring herself to work at Tracy Ross after Christmas. Firmly, Brenda said, "I work at Tracy Ross and I know he wasn't bothering anybody."

The policemen looked at each other, and the one with the mustache said, "Even so, we can't have him hanging around here. We'll see that he gets downtown. The shelter is dishing out free meals tonight."

Just the idea of a shelter sounded awful to Brenda. Before she could catch herself, Brenda said, "He's coming home with me."

"Are you sure?"

Brenda wasn't sure. In fact she was distressed by her own offer. Still, she couldn't see any way to back out now without looking like a complete fool. "I'm sure," she said.

The policemen wished her a merry Christmas and went away, leaving Brenda standing with Santa Bum on the deserted sidewalk.

Brenda asked, "Would you like to come home with me?"

"I'd love to if my reindeer can wait on your roof."

Brenda felt a little queasy. Was he just playing

with her, or did he really believe he was Santa
Claus? The policemen were gone. Brenda could
just cut and run. But if she did that, she would disappoint this perfectly harmless old man. Which
seemed unfair after her invitation.

Santa Bum told Brenda that his sleigh would
be coming from the North Pole later. She had to
pay bus fare for both of them, and Santa, his sack
riding between his feet, got a lot of stares from
the other riders. Even on Christmas Eve, the
sight of Santa riding a bus was not common, especially in Beverly Hills.

Brenda was self-conscious walking up her
own street. In the slanting winter sunlight, everything looked so normal. Only the guy walking
next to her struck a bizarre note.

While she and Santa walked up the street, he
admired the way people had decorated their houses. He had particular praise for the Walsh house.
"Plasterboard camels," he said. "Very nice. And
practical, too."

At the back door, Brenda stopped and took a
deep breath. She was apprehensive about what
her parents would say when she brought home a
stranger, even if he was Santa Claus. They would
have to understand that she'd had no other choice.

Brenda came into the kitchen and wished her
parents merry Christmas. They wished her
merry Christmas back and then were stunned
when they saw Santa Bum. They introduced
themselves and did not seem comforted when he

told them he was Santa Claus. Santa himself was as friendly as ever, entirely at ease with strangers. He wished everyone merry Christmas and handed out candy canes that he took from his sack.

"Excuse us," Mr. Walsh said and hustled Brenda into the dining room. Mrs. Walsh was right behind them.

"What's the story, Brenda?" Mr. Walsh asked.

"I found him on Rodeo Drive. Can he stay for dinner?"

Mrs. Walsh asked, "Who knows who's lurking under that beard?"

Her parents were asking all the questions she herself wanted answers to. Yet, now that she had made up her mind to take in this Santa person, the questions seemed irrelevant, perhaps even impolite. She said, "My instincts tell me he's harmless."

Mr. Walsh nodded and said sarcastically, "That makes me feel much better."

Before they had a chance to discuss Santa further, Kelly and her mom arrived and distracted everyone. Maybe her parents would have a chance to get used to the idea that Santa Bum was eating with them. Brenda hadn't quit gotten used to the idea yet herself, but you never knew.

Mr. and Mrs. Walsh were considerably more delighted to see Kelly and Mrs. Taylor than they had been to see Santa Bum. "I thought you were having Christmas dinner with David Silver and his dad," Mrs. Walsh said.

Mrs. Taylor lifted her nose and said disdainfully, "At the last minute, Mr. Silver decided to eat with his soon-to-be ex."

"I'm so sorry," Mrs. Walsh said and touched Mrs. Taylor's hand.

Mrs. Taylor shrugged and pretended to be unaffected. "I've survived worse," she said.

"Two more at the table, Jim," Mrs. Walsh said.

"Three," said Brenda.

Following a short uneasy silence, Mrs. Walsh said, "All right. Three."

Mr. Walsh did not look happy, but he said, "You got it," and went back into the kitchen.

Mrs. Walsh marveled at her company and said, "It's beginning to feel more like Christmas." She pinched Brenda's cheek and went back into the kitchen.

The only Christmas present Brenda wanted at the moment was for her little charitable act not to end in disaster.

Steve Sanders was still in Albuquerque, but he was working hard to get away. As he'd expected, all the commercial airlines were booked, and now he stood in the tiny office of Kringle Air, the only charter service with a light on this cold night. The cab driver who'd brought him said it might even snow.

The office was crowded with all kinds of airplane junk: paintings, photos, old calendars, old instruments, and piles of papers well thumbed with greasy fingerprints. Behind the desk was a lanky guy with a bell-shaped wart on the side of his nose. He was dressed in a Santa suit with black stains on the white cuffs and leaning back in a swivel chair watching "How the Grinch Stole Christmas" on TV.

The guy showed little interest in flying Steve to Los Angeles until Steve began throwing twenties onto his desk one at a time. "Stop me when I have your full attention," Steve said.

The guy's eyes got big and he asked Steve to stop unless he wanted to purchase an airplane. After some discussion, they agreed on a price—something less than what Steve had already thrown onto the desk—and the guy made his preparations.

It seemed to take forever for the guy to file his flight plan, check out his plane, and gas up. Eventually, Steve sat in the passenger seat listening to the guy gun the engine. "Let's go," Steve said impatiently.

The guy, still in his Santa suit, gave Steve the thumbs-up, and as the plane roared down the runway, he cried, "Now Dasher! now Dancer! now Prancer! now Vixen!"

Was the guy crazy? Maybe Steve should have just walked home, no matter how long it took.

The guy pulled back on the throttle, and like thistledown, the Rudolph rose into the air. "On, Comet! on, Cupid! on, Donder, and Blitzen!"

The guy hummed to himself. Steve settled down in his seat and closed his eyes. He tried to think about his mother, and not about the thousands of feet of empty air below them.

13

"Happy Christmas to all—"

MRS. WALSH DECIDED THAT A SIT-DOWN dinner was no longer practical, and she suggested a buffet. Nobody seemed to mind. "As long as there's food," Brandon said.

The guests circled the table, browsing among the steaming platters. Santa held a plate in one hand and dragged his sack with the other. The whole operation looked a little awkward to Brandon, so he asked if he could take the sack.

"No," said Santa pleasantly, "I'll just keep it with me if it's all the same to you."

Brandon hoped the guy wasn't a mad bomber. Or even an angry bomber.

The doorbell rang and Samantha Sanders

jumped like a startled deer. She put down her plate, called, "I'll get it," and was halfway to the front door before she realized that she wasn't in her own house.

"We'll both get it," Mrs. Walsh said, and put her arm through Mrs. Sanders's.

Brandon could see the disappointment on Mrs. Sanders's face when she opened the door on Andrea instead of on Steve. But she made a quick recovery and did her best to make Andrea feel welcome.

Andrea was carrying a roast pan covered in aluminum. "My grandmother sent a brisket."

"Sure," said Brandon, "the traditional Christmas brisket."

Andrea went pink, and Brandon saw his mistake. He put his arm around her shoulders and said, "Glad you could make it."

"Me, too. I mean, I've never been to a real Christmas dinner before. I can't wait to try some of that plum pudding."

Brandon made a face and said, "Oh, yuckers! I hate plum pudding."

But the truth was that plum pudding was one of the few things about Christmas that Brandon hated. He made do with turkey and stuffing and potatoes and cranberry sauce and puddles of gravy.

After no one could eat any more, Santa Bum pulled a box from his sack and handed it to Mrs. Walsh. "A little something for the hostess."

"That isn't—"

"Please," Santa Bum said.

Inside the box was a beautiful scarf, which Mrs. Walsh quickly draped around her neck.

In the living room, Santa gave a box to Brenda and one to Andrea. Mr. and Mrs. Walsh watched with growing suspicion as more expensive gifts were revealed. Brenda got a pair of earrings from Tiffany's, and Andrea got a genuine leather key ring imported from England.

Brenda looked at Andrea's present with interest and said, "We sell these at the store."

Mr. Walsh was growing grimmer by the moment, and Mrs. Walsh was finding it increasingly difficult to hide her alarm.

"You keep an eye on things here," Mrs. Walsh whispered to her husband, "I'm going to go count the silver." As she walked toward the stairs, the doorbell rang. "I'll get it," she called.

Brandon understood his parents' fears. He himself had his suspicions about the outfit their Santa was wearing. Had he stolen it from Nat the day he'd come into the Peach Pit looking for a handout? The possibility existed. Yet, Brandon wasn't even sure this was the same guy. And all Santa suits looked pretty much alike.

It was true that the guy was wearing a suspicious Santa suit, and that he didn't look prosperous enough to have purchased all those things, but as far as Brandon was concerned, it was a little early to accuse him of stealing. The way he pulled just the right gift from his sack for each person had a certain magical quality. Maybe it was just the Christmas spirit, but Brandon was inclined to give the guy some slack.

Mel Silver marched into the room looking earnest. He was a tall man wearing a dark suit along with his intense expression. His eyes looked huge behind his glasses. He was not the sex object Brandon would have expected Jackie Taylor to fall for, but stranger things had happened. Mr. Silver was followed by David, and then by Mrs. Walsh, who seemed concerned about what might happen next.

Mr. Silver stopped in the middle of the room and said, "Jackie, I want to say this in front of our friends so there will be no misunderstanding. I want witnesses."

Jackie was astonished to see Mel Silver, and then her face showed nothing at all. Coolly, she said, "Why, Mel. What a surprise."

Mr. Silver said, "Jackie, I made a stupid mistake." He pounded his chest with his fist. "I just want to tear out my heart."

"Have a good time," Mrs. Taylor said. "Excuse me. I have to powder my nose."

As she passed Mr. Silver, he unexpectedly grabbed her by the shoulders and said, "There's a point where when you separate, you just have to separate."

"I'm sorry it didn't work out."

Brandon could tell she wasn't.

"I never went," Mr. Silver said. "I just drove around and around, torturing myself, feeling like a jerk. And then it hit me: I love you, Jackie. I really do."

Mrs. Taylor's expression didn't change, and Mr. Silver kissed her full on the mouth. For a moment, Mr. Silver might as well have been kissing a wall. Then Mrs. Taylor melted into his embrace and returned the kiss. They broke but still held each other's arms. Mrs. Taylor kissed David on the cheek, and Mr. Silver kissed Kelly. They wished each other merry Christmas.

Mr. Silver and Mrs. Taylor looked into each other's eyes. Everybody was watching them. Had he been so inclined, Santa could have trucked out the TV set without anybody noticing.

The doorbell rang and Kelly cried, "I'll get it."

Brandon tried to get a grip on who was missing. If he didn't count Steve, it could be either Donna or Dylan; neither was a likely candidate. Then Santa handed Brandon a small box, and he forgot all about the bell. The box rattled. Inside was a pair of World War I dog tags on a chain. Brandon was awestruck. Some guy—Favere, Jack K.—had actually worn these into battle. The tags were just dripping with history. He held them up and said, "Wow!"

Donna came in and reported that there was no snow in Mammoth.

"That's great," Brenda said.

Brandon had to go to the bathroom. As he

walked to the stairway to the second floor, he passed Donna and David, who were regarding each other shyly.

"Watch where you're standing, Donna," Brandon said.

"Huh?" asked Donna.

Brandon pointed up at the sprig of mistletoe tacked to the doorway.

David leaned down to kiss Donna. She seemed to enjoy it, despite her embarrassment.

In the foyer, Mr. Walsh was saying good night to Mrs. Sanders, who was hurrying home to wait by the phone for Steve's call.

"Are you sure there's nothing we can do?" Mr. Walsh asked.

"Just pray that he's okay," Mrs. Sanders said. "And say good-bye to Cindy for me." She looked at Brandon with tears in her eyes. "Steve has some wonderful friends." She could not bring herself to say more, and she left abruptly.

Brandon climbed the stairs and went to the bathroom. On his way back, he was about to pass his parents' open door, when he heard them talking. They spoke like angry conspirators. Brandon was no better than human, so he stopped to listen.

Mrs. Walsh said, "He didn't touch the silver, but he took my engagement ring."

So, Brandon thought, Santa Bum was really Santa Crook.

"Is anything else missing?" Mr. Walsh asked.

"Not that I can see." Mrs. Walsh became angrier. "Brenda brings home some eccentric street person who's carrying a sackful of merchandise from the most expensive stores in Beverly Hills. What am I to think when I find my ring missing?"

"What are you doing?"

Dad sounded unaccountably nervous, as if Mom were accusing him of stealing the ring.

"I'm calling the police." She began to punch in numbers.

It seemed like a good move to Brandon. He knew he should warn the people downstairs that a felon was in their midst, but he wondered how to go about it without warning Santa.

14

"—And to all a good night!"

"PUT DOWN THE PHONE, DEAR," MR. WALSH said gently.

This development was entirely unexpected. There was no way for Brandon to move at the moment.

"What?" Mrs. Walsh asked. And then, even more puzzled, she asked, "What's this? My ring!"

"I took it over a week ago to have it reset."

"Oh, Jim, I love it."

"And I love *you*."

Brandon was not accustomed to thinking of his parents as romantic people, and the situation was getting a little steamy in any event. Embarrassed,

Brandon hightailed it downstairs. These people needed their privacy.

In the living room, Donna was explaining to Santa why Christmas bummed her out. Brandon had entirely forgotten, if he'd ever known, that Christmas was Donna's birthday. She rarely got two sets of presents and never got a party of her own.

Santa listened sympathetically and then began to sing the happy birthday song to Donna. Everyone joined in. Donna beamed.

Brandon couldn't figure this Santa guy out. If he wasn't the real Santa Claus, he was the next best thing, spreading joy wherever he went. Just for this one night, Brandon was ready to believe.

By the time they were done, Mr. and Mrs. Walsh had come downstairs, and Mrs. Walsh flashed her ring around. Mr. Walsh stood by proudly. Brandon sidled over next to him and punched him in the shoulder. "Good going, Dad."

"Yeah."

"So, you think that's really ol' Saint Nick, himself?"

Mr. Walsh shrugged. "Why not? He has to spend Christmas Eve somewhere, doesn't he?"

Sure. Why not the Walsh home? Made sense to Brandon. The big question was, where was Steve Sanders spending Christmas Eve?

The pilot sang Christmas songs all the way to Santa Monica Airport. Steve wasn't really in the mood, but if the singing calmed the guy and made him a better pilot, Steve wasn't going to argue.

Flying in a private plane at night was odd. Except for the occasional sudden dips and rises, during which Steve tried to control his stomach, it was almost like riding in an automobile. The cabin was very cold, and Steve was grateful to find a blanket behind his seat. The cold and the constant roar of the engine were the things Steve remembered most. The cold and the roar and the singing.

They flew over scattered lights, then the lights bunched together, then they strung out along streets. Los Angeles was huge, one continuous slab of concrete from San Bernardino to the sea, seventy or eighty miles. For the last twenty minutes of the flight, the plane dropped in shallow stair steps till they were so low that Steve thought they were going to tangle in telephone wires.

The descent made Steve a little woozy, and he was grateful when the plane landed at last and rolled to a stop. The pilot switched off the engine, and for a moment Steve thought he had gone deaf. Then he opened the door and was slapped in the face by air that seemed much warmer than the stuff aloft. Faraway traffic noise and the wasp sound of other planes taking off and landing assured him that he could still hear.

Steve was stiff when he got out of the plane and dropped to the ground. He and the pilot wished each other luck and a merry Christmas.

The pilot sauntered off looking for a hot cup of coffee; Steve staggered away to find a cab.

He had to call one, and it took a long time to arrive. It was the last cab he hoped to see the inside of for quite a while. Traffic was light, as it would be on Christmas Eve. Everybody was bundled in somewhere.

When he got home, Steve was surprised, and more than a little disappointed to find the place dark. He unlocked the door, called, "Mom?" and waited for an answer. None came. She had not even bothered to plug in the Christmas tree. Hell of a note. He returns from this big emotional adventure, and she goes out to party.

He plugged in the tree, and after appreciating the blinking lights for a moment, went upstairs. While he unpacked, he forgave her. After all, she didn't know when he was coming home, or even *if* he was coming home. He'd been a jerk to leave her on Christmas anyway. He could have waited till after New Year's to find his past. After seventeen years, what difference would another week make? Sure, it was easy to be smart now. He wondered if, by going when he did, he'd made a fatal error. Would this woman ever love him again?

He'd been doing too much thinking lately, and he needed to take his brain out of gear. He flopped onto his bed and using the remote, turned on the TV. He zapped from channel to channel until he found *Miracle on 34th Street*. He was please to see it was the black-and-white version, not the colorized one.

■   ■   ■

It was a gas, really. Andrea claimed that she'd never really done Christmas before, which was easy enough to believe. But now that she was here, Brandon was bemused to see how well she adjusted. The Christmas spirit seemed to have possessed her entirely. Santa made the mistake of asking her what she wanted for Christmas.

Andrea folded her hands in her lap as if reciting and said, "Even when I was a little girl, I never believed in Santa Claus. I thought it was pointless for me to ask him for anything because our house didn't have a chimney, and we never had a Christmas tree."

Brandon and the others watched with amazement as she rambled on. Even Santa seemed surprised and taken aback. The doorbell rang, and Brenda was the first to leap up and say, "I'll get it."

"But sitting here," Andrea said, "I feel like, you know, what the hell! Asking couldn't hurt. I want one of those notebook computers and some bubble bath, and I saw these great boots down at—"

A commotion in the foyer was followed by the entrance of Dylan. He had his arm across Brenda's shoulder, and she was carrying a bunch of flowers. Mr. and Mrs. Walsh walked behind. Mrs. Walsh still stole glances at her ring.

"Hey, bro," Brandon said. He was glad to see Dylan. Not as glad as Brenda was, maybe, but genuinely pleased. "How's your dad?"

Dylan shrugged. "Not bad for a guy in the can. He says he's doing a lot of thinking. Maybe he is." When he saw Santa, Dylan studied him for a moment and said, "Didn't I see you somewhere else tonight?" He rubbed the side of his nose, right where Santa's bell-shaped wart was.

"I don't think so. I've been here all evening."

Mr. and Mrs. Walsh settled onto the couch opposite him. Mrs. Walsh asked, "Who are you, really?"

Good question, Brandon thought. Evidently, everybody else thought so, too, because they all watched Santa and waited silently for his answer.

Santa smiled whimsically and said, "Why, I'm Santa Claus."

Mrs. Walsh said, "Well, if—"

Santa looked into the past and spoke as if explaining to himself as much as to them. "For over forty years I lived with Mrs. Claus in a big house high on a hill, and she made the most wonderful Christmas dinners. Much like the one we had tonight. We had a big tree and sleigh loads of presents for lots of little elves.

"But the elves grew up and moved away. After that, even though she and I were the only ones left, Mrs. Claus still made the most splendid Christmas dinners.

"Last year, Mrs. Claus died, and as far as I was concerned Christmas died with her. But something inside me told me to go looking for Christmas magic anyway. I searched as best I could, and for a long time found nothing but sorrow and the opportunity to spend the night in jail."

He stopped, smiled again, and stared benignly at Brenda. "Until that girl took a lonely old man home for dinner and allowed him to believe again in the spirit of Christmas."

Brandon wiped his eyes, and he saw others doing the same. There was nothing like a sad story with a happy ending to bring out the tears in everyone.

The spell was broken by the ringing of the doorbell.

Brandon said, "Must be a Girl Scout selling cookies. Everybody we know is here." He went to answer the door, and when he pulled it open was met by a group of carolers who exploded into an enthusiastic rendition of "We Wish You a Merry Christmas." In the middle of the group, singing with gusto, was Nat.

Brandon smiled broadly while he was joined by everybody in the house. When the song was over, everyone applauded. Mrs. Walsh invited Nat in for a drink. At first he declined because, he said, the carolers had a lot of houses to cover. "And we don't have any reindeer." He blinked when he saw Santa Bum.

"Come on, Nat, just one," Brandon said.

With only a little more coaxing Nat agreed to stay. "I'll catch up with you guys down the street," he called to the carolers as Mr. Walsh closed the door.

Nat wriggled with delight when he was given innocent Christmas kisses by Brenda, Kelly, and

Donna. He stared when Santa shook his hand and wished him a merry Christmas.

"By the way," Nat said as he turned to Brandon. "I found my Santa suit. One of the busboys stowed it under the counter where it would be 'safe.'" He held up his hands to put finger quotes around "safe."

Brandon turned to stare at Santa Bum, too. In the back of his mind he'd really assumed that the guy had stolen Nat's suit, and Brandon had long since forgiven him for it—obviously, the guy had a real talent for Santa-ing. But if the suit he wore didn't belong to Nat, where had he gotten it? And how true was that fairy tale about Mrs. Claus and the elves? Who was this guy?

Steve watched *Miracle on 34th Street* while fading in and out of sleep. Suddenly, his mom rushed into the room, and cried, "Steve!"

His mom! She looked flushed, as if she'd run up the stairs, but happy. He leapt to his feet. Despite the fact that he'd wanted to come home, wanted to see his mom again, he was surprised at the pleasure seeing her gave him.

"I've been waiting over an hour," he said. "You don't know what I went through to get here. I don't think you'll be so happy to see me when you find out what my little adventure cost."

She seemed not to have been listening but to be enchanted by his very existence. She said, "Shut up and hug me."

Steve hugged her tightly. Few things had ever felt so right. He knew he'd been talking too much, but he could not help himself. Equal parts of excitement and relief energized him. "I had to go. I had to find out where I came from and what my real mother was like."

Mrs. Sanders thought about that for a moment and then asked, "Was she everything you expected?"

"Everything and more."

"I see." Reluctantly, Mrs. Sanders let go of him. She sat on the end of the bed, her hands in her lap.

Steve could not stand to see her so dejected, so he said, "Let me tell you about her. She's beautiful and caring, and she created me out of her love—seventeen years of it."

Mrs. Sanders looked up at him and smiled tentatively.

"With everything going on in her life," Steve said, "she always tried to teach me to do the right thing. And she was always there for me when I made mistakes. And no matter what, she always let me know how much she really loved me."

Mrs. Sanders was grinning now and wiping away tears. Steve was glad to see she'd gotten the message. He said, "I'm sorry I had to go so far away to find you, Mom."

They hugged again. Mrs. Sanders said, "Oh, Gorgeous, I'm just glad you're back."

"Me, too. And I promise you one thing."

"What's that?"

"I'll never leave you on Christmas again." And he wouldn't. The promise he made to himself was even more important than the promise he made to his mom.

Mr. Walsh came up next to Brandon and whispered, "How are we doing?"

"Ready any time you are, Dad."

"Zero hour," Mr. Walsh said, and gave Brandon a thumbs-up. While Brandon headed for the front door, Mr. Walsh called, "Gather around the organ, everyone. We'll sing some carols of our own."

Brandon closed the front door on his dad launching into "White Christmas."

Brenda was always embarrassed when her dad tried to entertain by playing the organ, but she decided that part of her gift to him this year would be that she wouldn't complain. Everyone was singing when suddenly Mrs. Walsh gripped her husband's shoulder, and she pointed out the front window as if she'd seen Marley's ghost.

"Oh my gosh," Brenda cried. It was snowing! Flurries of actual snow were falling past their front window. Impossible. Yet there it was. Everyone continued to sing, now with renewed fervor, encouraged by the snow. Snow! Brenda couldn't get over it. A white Christmas indeed!

■ ■ ■

Brandon checked all the connections on the snowblower one more time, and then stood back to enjoy the effect. The machine took in water delivered by the garden hose, froze it, and spewed ice crystals—snow—into the air. The snow fell nicely in front of the living-room window and was making a drift on the grass. Through the window, Brandon could see Mrs. Walsh grinning. So all their trouble had been worthwhile. This was a Christmas she would never forget.

Behind him a horn honked. Brandon turned to see Steve pulling into the driveway in his Corvette. His mom sat next to him. They both seemed to be happy. Great news. Brandon had been worried that even if Steve came back in one piece, his experience would have changed him in ways none of them would like. Apparently, *not*.

Steve leaped from his car, ran around and opened the door for his mom. She got out and made a little curtsy. They were evidently in a playful mood.

"Hey, man," Brandon called.

"Hey, man," Steve called. "White Christmas, huh?"

"You bet. Good to see you." They shook hands.

Mrs. Sanders said, "Can you believe it? He was waiting for me when I got home."

"And you know what, Brandon? I'm starving."

"You came to the right place, bro. Free food inside." Brandon checked the snowblower one more time, and went into the house with them.

For the first time, Brandon had a chance to see what the falling snow looked like from inside the house. Very convincing, if he did say so himself.

Mr. Walsh was still leading "White Christmas" from the organ. Steve loaded up his plate and went into the living room, where people were paired off: Mrs. Walsh gazed out the window in wonderment with her hand still on her husband's shoulder. David and Donna had their arms around each other, as did Brenda and Dylan, Jackie and Mel. Though Brandon still didn't want to make a commitment to Andrea, he saw nothing wrong with holding her hand.

When Kelly saw Steve, she gasped and ran to him. She forced him to put down his plate of food so she could hug him properly. Steve gaped at Santa, and he was about to say something, but Santa winked at him like a conspirator, and Steve only nodded.

They all sang, "'. . . and may all your Christmases be white!'" They held the last note for a long time, and then gave themselves enthusiastic applause. There was a round of merry Christmas wishes.

And it was always said of the Walshes, that they knew how to keep Christmas well, if any family alive possessed the knowledge. May that be truly said of us, and all of us!

And as Brandon observed, "God bless us, every one."

Go back to the beginning...
See the 90 minutes that started it all!

THE BEVERLY HILLS, 90210 HOME VIDEO
"THE PILOT EPISODE"
AVAILABLE WHEREVER VIDEOS ARE SOLD